FIRESIDE GHOST STORIES

by A.S. Mott

Ghost House Books

First printed in 2003 10 9 8 7 6 5 4 3 2 1
Printed in Canada

The Publisher: Ghost House Books
Distributed by Lone Pine Publishing

10145 – 81 Avenue
Edmonton, AB T6E 1W9
Canada

1808 – B Street NW, Suite 140
Auburn, WA
USA 98001

Website: http://www.ghostbooks.net

National Library of Canada Cataloguing in Publication
Mott, A.S., 1975–
Fireside ghost stories / A.S. Mott.

ISBN 1-894877-40-3

1. Ghosts. I. Title.
GR580.M68 2003 398.25 C2003-904900-0

Editorial Director: Nancy Foulds
Project Editors: Shelagh Kubish, Dawn Loewen
Production Manager: Gene Longson
Cover Design: Curtis Pillipow
Layout & Production: Lynett McKell

The stories, folklore and legends in this book are based on the author's collection of sources including individuals whose experiences have led them to believe they have encountered phenomena of some kind or another. They are meant to entertain, and neither the publisher nor the author claims these stories represent fact.

We acknowledge the financial support of the Government of Canada through the Book Publishing Industry Development Program (BPIDP) for our publishing activities.

PC: P1

To M. & D.
This one seems real enough.

Contents

Acknowledgments

Since, like most writers, I cannot be bothered with such mundane details as proper spelling, punctuation and using words that actually exist, I am indebted to the efforts of my editor, Shelagh Kubish. Though her harsh and cruel words frequently brought me to tears and made me question the wisdom of my ever being born, I suspect that most of the time she was acting out of an impulse to improve the book and not just to glory in the spectacle of my humiliation. Seriously, she was great, even if she vetoed my use of a popular and fairly benign curse word.

I would also like to thank Dawn Loewen for her ideas and insights.

Because this book is fictional, I was beholden to come up with names for the characters in my stories. To do this I cheated a bit and ended up stealing quite a few from my extended family. I just want to say now that—with the exception of the character named after my cousin Mark—these names were employed completely randomly. So if you are related to me and find your name in this book, then please do not assume that the traits of the character who shares your name are meant in any way to be a statement about your own personality—unless, as I stated above, your name is Mark. Also, if your name does not appear in this book, please do not be offended by the omission. Hopefully, they'll let me do this again sometime and if so you'll have another chance to be (mis)represented.

I also would like to thank Lynett McKell, who put this book together, and Curtis Pillipow, who designed the cover.

Finally I have to thank Nancy Foulds and Shane Kennedy for giving me the opportunity to work on my first work of published fiction. This is an important milestone in my life, and words cannot describe what it means to me.

Introduction

One of the great truisms of the publishing world is that if the writers had complete control over the product, then the industry would be completely bankrupt within a week. In the name of truth and art, our first impulses often run against the current of good marketing in a way that can only be described as insanely self-destructive.

I bring this up because, if I had my way, this book would be called *Stories of Loneliness and Isolation*, which is—from a marketing standpoint—an appallingly awful title. It is the sort of title that people run screaming from, afraid that its pretentious melancholy might be contagious. It was only when I was close to finishing this book that I realized that so many of the stories dealt with the subject of loneliness and isolation. Thanks to my notions of what is scary in this world, and the fact that I wrote these stories when I myself was alone and isolated from the world, this strikes me as eerily appropriate.

Through movies, books and television shows, I've had years of exposure to popular culture's interpretations of ghosts and monsters. It is because of this exposure that I find little about these supposedly frightening creatures to be frightening.

Instead, I am made anxious by the more real and mundane dangers of life, and it is thanks to this that the real monsters in these stories are not the ghosts that inhabit them, but the pain of helplessness and the thought that once you are in the dark, you'll never see the light again.

In fact there are only a handful of characters in this book whom I would describe as evil, as the suspense and tension comes not from acts of malicious intent, but rather incidents of random disaster. The result of this is, I think, a book that is both thrilling and scary, but—in a strange way—comforting as well. The stories seem to suggest that it really is darkest before the dawn and that all it takes to be brave is a little patience and some faith.

Whether this is true or not is a subject that can easily be debated. I suggest that—as this book's actual title suggests—you sit down in a comfortable chair in front of a nice warm fire and decide for yourself.

In His Head

Much to the chagrin of his wife, Shirley, Laurence had been staying up later and later. "Go to sleep," she would scold him while he sat beside her on their bed, reading anything he could find, late into the night. At that point he would usually put down his book or magazine, turn off the lamp on his bedside table and lie down, but he seldom went to sleep. He would lie beside her in the dark for hours, listening to her gentle snores and the creaks and moans of their house, until, at last, exhaustion would take over and force him to dream.

He was too ashamed to tell anyone about the nightmares. He was 66, a grandfather and a well-respected businessman with a den full of awards for all the charity work he had performed throughout his life, and it embarrassed him greatly that a few scary dreams could make him feel like a frightened child. He couldn't understand where the dreams came from. His life had been quiet and tranquil. He had been spared the terrors of war, had never known poverty and had enjoyed a childhood free of any abuse. There were no demons in his past, but night after night demons would infect his dreams to the point that he was beginning to question his sanity.

The night before had been the worst so far. He had dreamed that the people he loved had come over to celebrate his birthday, but he couldn't experience it with them. He sat in his favorite chair in the living room, and his children and grandchildren went up to him and talked to him, but he couldn't say anything back to them. Instead he just sat there, the right side of his face slack and motionless, incapable of any expression. He would try to respond, but the words would not come and his thoughts would stay trapped in his head, forever unexpressed. While he found this disturbing, what scared him even more was the black shape he could see floating among his family. It had no distinct features beyond its blackness, which looked as though it could steal the light of even the brightest star. Laurence knew that the shape was evil and that its intention was to harm his family, and he tried to warn them that it was there, but the words stayed trapped in his mind, unable to make it to his lips. He was forced to sit and watch as the blackness engulfed his loved ones and turned their hearts cold and their words sharp. His children and grandchildren screamed at each other. Shirley yelled at them all and told them that she would sooner die than talk to any of them again. He could see the blackness grow, as words became fists and his family began to physically fight each other in front of him. He still could not move and was forced to watch as they killed each other and as the blackness overtook the entire house. It was only as the blackness came upon him that he was able to make a sound. He screamed and screamed and awoke himself from the horror he had just experienced.

This night he sat beside Shirley and tried to read a novel about a young lawyer who gets in trouble with his sinister clients, but he couldn't get into it. Like clockwork, Shirley scolded him to go to sleep and he dutifully turned off the light. He lay down and turned his head to look out his bedroom window. The moon was full and bright and it illuminated their room enough that he could have continued reading if he'd wanted to, but instead he left his book on his nightstand and thought of all the happy times he had spent with his family. Trying to understand what could make him dream what he dreamed, he thought back and tried to remember if there was ever a moment when it felt as though their love and happiness felt like a sham—like a ruse perpetrated by the family to make their lives easier. But no such moment existed. His family's love was real, he was sure, and his dream made no sense.

His thoughts drifted as he stared at the moon. It really was like a big pizza pie, he decided. Dean Martin really knew what he was singing about. Remembering that song made him think about the time he and Shirley danced to it, 45 years ago. He'd proposed to her that night. She had looked beautiful in a pink dress her mother had made, and he tried his best to look handsome in a suit handed down to him from his older brother. She had sensed that he was nervous but hadn't guessed why, so she was truly surprised when he got down on one knee and handed her the ring he had bought. He closed his eyes and remembered the joy he had felt when she said yes to him as quickly as she could, afraid that even the slightest hesitation might offend him. He closed his eyes and remembered and saw a black floating shape behind her.

He opened his eyes and sat up straight in his bed. He was terrified to realize that the shape was now invading his thoughts as well as his dreams. He looked out the window and tried to take comfort in the moonlight. It was then that he felt a strange tingle throughout his body. Although he was hot enough to be sweating, his body began to shiver. His head began to throb with a sharp burning pain he had never felt before. A fire began to rage inside his mind. It was then that from the light outside his window he could see that he and Shirley were not alone in their room. There, floating at the foot of their bed, he could see a black shape.

He screamed.

His screams woke Shirley, who turned on her light and watched as her husband clasped his hands to his head. She watched as he collapsed beside her and became horribly silent.

* * *

The doctor's prognosis wasn't good.

"I'm afraid your husband has had a stroke," he explained to Shirley, who was doing her best to look brave as she held the hand of her oldest daughter, Bethany. The doctor went on to explain that the stroke had occurred in the front left-hand side of Laurence's brain. "While it's too early to tell what effect this will have on him, chances are good that he will suffer some form of paralysis, as well as memory loss and aphasia."

"Aphasia?" asked Calvin, their third son.

"It means he may find it difficult to communicate. Each case tends to be unique. Some people are rendered permanently mute, while others get their speech back right away. In other cases people can talk just fine, but they have difficulty understanding what is said to them. But until he wakes up, we'll have no idea how bad his is, if he even suffers from it, that is."

"Do you have any idea why this happened?" This came from Hank, their oldest son.

"There are a lot of different factors, but in your father's case we suspect that his high blood pressure was the leading cause."

"High blood pressure? Laurence didn't have high blood pressure," Shirley insisted.

"Not according to our tests," answered the doctor.

"But he ate well, he exercised, he did everything he had to do to keep it down."

"Do you know if he was experiencing any stress?" asked the doctor.

Shirley shook her head. "I don't think so. Although he wasn't getting much sleep at night."

Several hours later Laurence was taken into surgery and the doctors worked to relieve pressure on his brain. He remained unconscious for some time afterward, but when he finally woke up, Shirley was right beside him.

He looked at her and tried to speak, but he couldn't get any words to come out of his mouth. He wanted to tell her that he loved her and that he felt okay, but his thoughts refused to leave his brain.

Shirley noticed that he was awake and gently kissed him on the cheek.

"Don't do that again," she whispered sweetly to him.

He tried to smile at her, but he could get only the left half of his face to work. The right side felt numb and he couldn't move it at all. He tried to lift up his right hand to touch her cheek, but it too was paralyzed. His body was so sore he could barely lift up his left hand, but at least it seemed to work. Unable to speak, all he could do was listen as Shirley explained to him what the doctor had told her and how their children were doing.

He watched her and was frightened by how scared she looked. It crushed him to realize that he was causing her so much pain. He began to worry about whether she was capable of handling the emotional and financial strain without him. None of this inner turmoil registered on his face. He looked at the woman he had been married to for 45 years with a blank expression, when he would have happily given anything to let her know with a single look how much he loved her and needed her.

Laurence had never been inside a jail, so he had never before felt the sensation of being locked away from all that he cared about, but he recognized it now. He felt as though he had been thrown into the coldest and darkest cell in the world and that the prison was his own body.

A nurse came in and told Shirley that she had to leave. Visiting hours were over and Laurence needed his rest. Laurence wanted her to stay—he needed her to stay—but he remained silent and motionless as she gathered her things, said good-bye and walked out the door.

A machine was connected to Laurence that measured his pulse. Each beep the machine emitted indicated a different heartbeat, and so far its rhythm had been slow and steady, but as he watched his wife leave the beeps came faster and faster, until they rose to a dangerous and heart-stopping level. The nurse who had told Shirley to leave immediately rushed over to the room's intercom and ordered an emergency crew to rush to Laurence's side. They were there within a minute and successfully lowered his heart rate and kept him from having a heart attack. When it was over the doctors were dumbfounded as to what might have caused this near fatal incident. Laurence was as fit and healthy as men 20 years his junior and there was nothing wrong with his heart.

What they did not know—what he could not tell them—was that when Shirley walked out of his room, he had seen that she was followed by a dark and ominous black shape.

After Laurence's near heart attack, the doctors insisted that he stay at the hospital longer than they had originally suggested. Despite their best efforts, something was keeping his blood pressure dangerously high and his heart rate erratic.

As more and more of his family members came to visit him, Laurence discovered that they were all being followed by the same black shape. He soon managed to control his terror whenever he was confronted by it, but the stress of not being able to warn his family was keeping him from going home. It was when he finally realized that he wasn't going to go home until he learned to control this stress that he made an effort to keep himself calm. Even though he knew nothing about meditation, he used its principles to control his heart rate. Instead of being a word, his mantra was the idea that he had to stay alive so he could get better, relearn to talk and warn his family. This goal eventually became the only thing he thought about and within a week his vital signs became steady enough that it was decided it was safe for him to go home.

His entire family was there when the orderly wheeled him outside. In front of them was a brand-new wheelchair wrapped up in a big red bow. Together the orderly and Hank lifted Laurence out of the hospital's wheelchair and into his own. Everyone hugged him and told him how happy they were that he was coming home, while he repeated his mantra over and over again in his head. It kept him calm while he watched the blackness follow everyone he loved.

Laurence was trying his best, but so far his physiotherapy wasn't helping him at all. The right side of his body was still paralyzed and his left side was still weak. Not only could he not walk, but he also didn't even have the strength to lift himself out of his chair.

The same was true for his speech exercises. No matter how hard he tried he could not get his lips and tongue to vocalize his thoughts, and so far the best he could manage was a quiet grunting noise that so embarrassed him he preferred to remain silent rather than make it.

Shirley was required to look after him almost 24 hours a day, which she did without complaint. Their children did everything they could to help her, but the responsibility rested squarely on her shoulders, and if she felt the strain she did not show it. When she talked to him she refused to acknowledge his silence and she guessed his responses and spoke them aloud herself. It moved Laurence to learn that nine times out of ten she was able to guess exactly what he wanted to say. It hurt him that the one time out of ten when she was wrong was when he wanted to tell her about the danger she was in. In his head he repeated his mantra and stayed convinced that in the end he would be able to protect her.

That is, until the shape started talking to him.

He didn't recognize it at first. The sound was distant and vague, like the rustling of a far-off wind. It was a soft sibilant sound, and when he first heard it he assumed it was another symptom of the stroke, but then as he sat and listened to it for days and days he began to be able to make out words in the seemingly random hum. Finally, a month after he started hearing the sound, he could understand what it said, and it almost killed him.

Shirley was there when it happened and immediately noticed her husband's distress. Within minutes an ambulance was parked in front of his house. The paramedics were able to slow down his heart rate, and they took him back to the hospital where a series of tests proved that he was in the same condition he'd been in when he left.

As strong as Laurence's mantra was in calming his fear, it was no match for what he heard that day.

The voice was quiet and confident. It didn't sound evil as much as it did certain, and its words nearly stopped his heart.

"Laurence," it whispered, "I am going to kill them. And you are going to watch me do it."

From then on the shape taunted Laurence during his every waking and dreaming moment. It told him in detail what it planned to do to his family and how it was going to make them tear each other apart in front of him.

"They will become animals, Laurence," it whispered to him. "Their savagery will be unlike anything the world has ever seen."

Shirley became concerned about the number of times she found tears in her husband's eyes.

"Don't worry, honey," she comforted him once while she held him. "I know how lonely and frustrating this must be for you, but I promise you we'll get through this."

Listening to her, Laurence felt for a moment that she could be right, but the shape quickly dispelled his optimism.

"She can make all the promises she wants, but they won't keep her alive."

Laurence did everything he could to try to communicate with the shape, but he was as mute to it as he was to the rest of the world. He desperately wanted to know why it took so much pleasure in his suffering and why it was so intent on destroying his family, but to this end the shape gave him no hints and only continued to describe the horror of what was to come.

Never a religious man, Laurence began to pray for a miracle. He prayed to be healed and to be able to walk out of his chair and talk to his family and warn them about what was to come, but his prayers went unanswered and he remained wordless and still. He tried to speak, hoping that somewhere in his grunts and groans someone would be able to hear his message, but no one ever understood him.

The days passed, refusing to slow down, until one night Shirley said the words he had dreaded for so long.

"Guess what, honey?" she said sweetly, unaware of the disaster she was foretelling. "It's your birthday tomorrow, and everyone is coming to see you. Isn't that wonderful?"

"Yes, Laurence," the shape whispered, "isn't it?"

Laurence did not sleep that night. He hoped that if he stayed awake then morning would not come and his nightmare would not be able to come true. But the sun still rose and Shirley woke up and buzzed around excitedly as she got the house ready. This was the type of day she lived for, and she had looked forward to it for weeks now.

At around noon, Hank and his family arrived and they helped her get Laurence ready. They fed him and dressed him in his nicest suit. Hank took him out of his wheelchair and sat him down in his favorite chair in the living room. He was there for only 10 minutes when the rest of Laurence's family—including his brothers and sisters and nieces and nephews—and his closest friends began to arrive. As soon as everyone walked in they headed straight to him and wished him a happy birthday, and every time they did the shape would tell him how they were going to die. When his daughter Sylvia kissed his cheek, the shape told him that her older brother Hank was going to snap her neck, and when his son Calvin gave his father a hug, the shape told him that Shirley herself would be the one to stab him in the heart with a butcher knife.

Laurence's heart began to pound faster and faster every time the doorbell rang and someone new came inside, but the terror truly took hold of him when the doorbell became silent and the last of the guests had arrived. This, he knew, was the moment the shape had been waiting for.

"It's time, Laurence," the shape announced to him, and to prove it, it grew and grew until it covered the entire house. "It's too bad that you can't say good-bye."

Then, just as in his dreams, the many little conversations in the house suddenly turned dark and accusatory. Angry words were shouted and tempers flared. Laurence watched helplessly as everyone he loved screamed at each other, as their fury escalated with each harsh word and their emotional violence edged quickly towards the physical kind.

Until that moment Laurence had kept himself alive by believing that he would somehow be freed from his prison and allowed to somehow stop the shape, but as he watched his nightmare unfold in front of him he knew that that wasn't going to happen. There would be no miracle cure and he would never recover in time to save them. Inside his head he screamed and roared and cried, despairing a fate he didn't know why he deserved. He watched as the first punches were thrown and the battle began. He closed his eyes and hoped that it would be over quickly.

It was only when Laurence gave up that he realized what he had to do. He had been so convinced that he had to be freed from his prison to save his family that it had never occurred to him that there was another option.

He could escape from it instead.

It was then that a miracle occurred. For the first time since his stroke, Laurence smiled. He smiled and his heart exploded.

Strength surged through him and he jumped out of his chair, his fists clenched in rage. He felt as if he were 20 again, and he screamed with an anger he had never felt before.

"Show yourself!" he raged. "Show yourself now!"

Everything froze around him. His family stopped moving and stiffened as if they had been turned to stone. The clock on the wall stopped ticking, and the fish in the tank stopped swimming.

Slowly the blackness of the shape began to diminish and contract. Its darkness faded and colors formed inside it. Its formlessness ceased as curves and contours became more recognizably human until finally Laurence saw a man standing in front of him. The man was small and flabby. He looked young, but he was already balding. He wore thick glasses that were decades out of style and his clothes looked as though they belonged in the pictures in Shirley and Laurence's high school yearbook.

Before the man could speak, Laurence ran to him and hit him as hard as he could. The man crumpled on the ground and began to cry. Laurence wanted to hit him some more, but he looked too pathetic lying there on the ground.

"Who are you?" he shouted at the man.

The man looked up at him. "Don't you know?"

Laurence stared at him and still had no idea who the man was.

"You don't, do you?"

Laurence shook his head.

"Typical!" The man pounded the floor in anger. "I spend decades planning and waiting to exact my revenge on you and you can't even remember who I am!"

For a moment, Laurence almost felt guilty about this, but he stopped himself and looked coldly at the man.

"Who are you, then?"

"I'm Jonathan Forster."

"Who?"

"Jon-a-than For-ster," the man repeated slowly and angrily.

Laurence tried to think back and couldn't recall anyone by that name, much less anyone with a reason to want to murder his entire family.

Jonathan grew annoyed by Laurence's silent attempt at recollection and impatiently explained, "I was Shirley's first boyfriend."

"No," Laurence gaped. "You?"

"Yes," Jonathan hissed.

"But you're an ugly little toad. She would have been way out of your league."

"I know," Jonathan admitted bitterly, "but there was a time when she didn't know that. Until she met you, that is. You took her away from me. She was all I had that was worth anything, and you took her away. I had nothing to live for after that. I shot myself the day you were married and when the bullet killed me I stepped out of my body and vowed that someday I would take away everything you had that should have been mine."

Laurence looked at Jonathan for a second before he grabbed him and lifted him off the ground. Jonathan's feet dangled helplessly in the air as Laurence looked him straight in the eye.

"You failed," he whispered to the frightened little man, "and if you come near my family ever again I will hurt you so badly you'll find out if there's an afterlife for the afterlife."

With that he threw Jonathan to the ground. Jonathan looked up at him and saw the fire in his eyes and knew that he was serious. Shamefully he bowed his head and slowly faded out of sight.

Instantly the world unfroze, and Laurence's family found themselves literally at each other's throats. Confused, they put each other down and dropped the cutlery and furniture they had been brandishing as weapons. Everyone started to apologize to each other as they all tried to comprehend what had just happened to them. Bandages were dispensed to those who had gotten cut, and ice was given to those who had sustained bruising. As everyone was being cared for, Hank went to check on his father, who remained seated in his favorite chair.

Laurence sat motionless. A smile lit up his face.

It fell to Calvin to deliver his father's eulogy. Hank had tried to do it, but when the moment came he found himself too overcome to speak. Calvin had little experience with public speaking, so as he read the last paragraph of his older brother's handwritten notes he sounded nervous and hesitant.

"My father was a great man. He was a kind man. A gentle man. But most of all he was a family man. Despite his successes in business and in the community, I know that his greatest happiness came from his success at being a father. As difficult as his passing is for me to accept, it makes me happy to know that he died while everyone he loved surrounded him. I know that of all the ways he could choose to die, that would be the one that he picked.

And now that he has passed on, he is the one who surrounds us. I take much comfort in the knowledge that wherever my father is now, he's watching over us and making sure we're okay."

With that Calvin folded up the piece of paper that his brother had given him and he stepped away from the altar. Then everyone said a prayer before they began to file out of the chapel and move on to the cemetery.

Laurence didn't follow them. He stayed in the chapel and thought about what Calvin had said. Tears filled his eyes as a great joy overcame him. They knew he was there. They knew he was watching over them, and they knew that he wouldn't allow anything bad to ever happen to them again.

The Cellar Dwellers

Clink. Clink. Clink. Clink. Clink.

Ishmael looked up from the musty old book he held in front of him, a simple volume dedicated to the art of catching rats. It was the only thing to read in the basement. Over the past 98 years, he had read it 2747 times. It had gotten to the point that he actually had the entire text memorized, but he enjoyed pretending that he had never seen it before and always acted as though he was discovering it for the first time. His act took some concentration, so he found the noise coming from his cellar-mate irritatingly distracting.

"What are you doing now?" he asked Cedric—who appeared to be methodically tapping an exposed pipe with a small wrench—but Cedric was far too engrossed to respond. He kept on clinking.

Clink. Clink. Clink. Clink. Clink.

Ishmael sighed and rolled his eyes. He and Cedric had been stuck together so long that he had become used to the scruffy little man's bizarre experiments. He looked back at him and saw that his tongue was hanging out of his mouth as he rhythmically tapped the pipe.

"Cedric!" he shouted. "Put that disgusting pink thing away at once!"

This got Cedric's attention. His tongue popped back into his mouth. "What?" he asked innocently, annoyed by Ishmael's rude interruption.

"Why are you tapping on that pipe?" Ishmael asked wearily, positive that he didn't want to hear the answer.

"I had an idea!" Cedric answered brightly.

"Yes?"

"I thought that the reason it's been so long since the old lady came down here is because she's had no reason to, so I figured if I started banging on this pipe she'd hear it and decide that she had to investigate or—better yet—send down a repairman." Cedric's face flushed at his own brilliance.

"That's your idea, is it?" asked Ishmael.

"Yep!" Cedric smiled happily.

"You do realize that there is a flaw in your reasoning, don't you?"

"Pardon?"

"It's not going to work."

"Why not?"

"Because," Ishmael sighed, "the old lady has not come down here for 40 years."

"So?"

"There is a reason we call her the old lady," Ishmael explained as if he were speaking to a particularly stupid child, "and that is because she is old, or I should say *was* old, because I guarantee you that she is—like us—most certainly deceased."

"You don't know that," Cedric protested.

"Not for a fact, that's true. But I do know enough about human physiology to say that the chances of her having lived to the ripe old age of 120 are rather remote."

Cedric thought about this. "I had a great-great-uncle who lived to 99" was the best argument he could come up with.

Ishmael put down his book.

"She's dead, Cedric. I suggest you get over it."

"But I'm so bored!" Cedric whined. "There's nothing to do down here. It used to be great. The old lady would come down and we'd make—"

"Excuse me?"

"All right," Cedric corrected himself, "*I'd* make scary noises and move things around on her and she'd get all nervous and run back upstairs. Those were good times. I miss them."

"I do not doubt that you do, but I am afraid that your problem is not going to be solved by banging—"

Before Ishmael could finish his sentence, he was interrupted by the sound of the cellar door being pulled open. The two ghosts looked up and watched as a handsome man poked his head into the doorway.

"That's strange," the man said to someone behind him. "Now I don't hear it."

Ishmael Amis had been a well-known academic. A history professor, he had specialized in the study of ancient Rome and had spent much of his time on the lecture circuit promoting the novels he wrote based on his studies. His first two books had been mild successes, but his third—which followed his publisher's suggestions to place more of its emphasis on sex and violence than on historical accuracy—was a runaway bestseller. Thanks to the comfortable living he made from his royalties he was able to quit teaching and work on his writing full time. With his lovely young daughter, Gwendolyn, he moved into the finest house in Braggsville, Massachusetts, a house on the corner of Winslow and Vine.

Cedric O'Neil was the son of Irish immigrants who had come to Boston in the hopes of a better life. Unlike many of their peers who had done the same, the O'Neils actually found what they were looking for. Cedric's father, Duncan, had exactly the type of chutzpah it took for an illiterate laborer to transform himself into a shrewd businessman. For the first three years that they lived in Boston, Duncan took every job he could find—often working up to 120 hours a week. Against the wishes of his wife, Catherine, he invested the money he made in a range of dubious schemes. She stopped nagging him, though, when it became clear that he knew what he was doing and his investments began to double and triple in value. Within 10 years Duncan O'Neil was one of the wealthiest men on the East Coast.

His son, however, did not inherit his father's gift for commerce. In fact, beyond an obvious physical resemblance, the two had nothing in common. Duncan was bright and hardworking, while Cedric was simple and lazy. He couldn't understand why people would spend a day at work when they could go to a pub and gamble and dance with pretty girls. When he was still a teenager he had already gained a reputation as one of Boston's most infamous libertines (although, in his defense, it didn't take much to develop a reputation in his highly conservative hometown).

Duncan despaired about what he was going to do with his rambunctious offspring and decided that his best option was to just get him out of town.

"If he's going to be a drunkard," Duncan told his wife, "let him do it out of our sight."

Duncan's first inclination was to send Cedric out of state, but Catherine insisted that her only son remain close enough for them to get to him if something horrible happened to him—for example, if he got stabbed in the throat during a bar brawl or shot in the stomach by an enraged husband. It was then that Duncan remembered that he had donated some money to a small college in the town of Braggsville.

"You're going to St. Catherine's Catholic Teachers College," he informed Cedric the next day.

In response, his son stared at him with a look of profound horror on his face. He tried to speak, but the words would not come.

"Don't worry," Duncan sighed, "I don't expect you to actually learn anything there."

With this said the terror vanished from Cedric's visage and he regained the ability to speak.

"Then why are you sending me?"

"Because it sounds better to tell people that I'm sending you off to be a teacher than to say that I'm sending you off to drink yourself to death," his father answered.

"Oh, okay, that makes sense," Cedric agreed cheerfully.

Cedric had never been to Braggsville, but he was optimistic enough to believe that it could be a fun place to live. Unfortunately his optimism proved to be misconceived, as there were few places as boring and lifeless. He was horrified to discover that alcohol was prohibited within the city's limits and that its populace was made up almost entirely of hardworking, God-fearing simple folk who disdained the pleasures of the flesh. The situation was so desperate that he actually found himself going to his classes, since there was nothing better to do. It was there that he met a young woman named Gwendolyn Amis.

Ishmael had no reason to disapprove of his daughter's newest suitor. The boy was dumb as a post, that was obvious, but he seemed polite and studious and was—according to Gwendolyn—the heir to a large fortune. This fact alone was enough for Ishmael to overlook the possibility of witless grandchildren, so he happily encouraged the relationship.

He did not realize that the reason his daughter was so infatuated with the boy from Boston was that she had sensed in him the reckless spirit that had gotten him banished from home. It was a spirit that also lay within her—one that she had long fought to control, but which she now longed to set free. When they were alone she would pester him to tell her stories about his carousing and the wild pranks he pulled on both his friends and his enemies. And as he told the same stories over and over again, she would listen with rapt attention and imagine herself in his place. One afternoon, as they sat together in her father's living room, she could take no more and told Cedric a secret she had kept for quite some time.

"Last year I traveled with Father while he went on his last book tour," she told him, "and when we were in New York, I"—she looked around nervously and leaned in to whisper to him—"stole a bottle of wine from a restaurant." She started to blush, but there was a strange pride in her voice. "I hid it in my closet. Do you"—she looked around once again—"do you want to come upstairs and drink it with me?"

This was not a question Cedric had to think about. "Yes," he answered, "yes I do."

Ishmael had been out when this conversation took place. He had been taking his daily walk about town, getting some sun and exchanging greetings with his neighbors. By the time he got back, Cedric and Gwendolyn were well on their way to insobriety.

Strangely, despite his vast experience with every sort of liquor and spirit a person could name, it took very little to get Cedric drunk. Gwendolyn, in contrast, had never before tasted alcohol and was still more lucid than he was as she matched him swallow for swallow. A thrilling warmth throbbed through her body and she giggled giddily as he attempted to tell her a joke, even though it was obvious that he had forgotten both the setup and the punch line. They were having so much fun that they didn't hear her father come back.

Ishmael, on the other hand, had no problem hearing what was going on upstairs. As soon as he walked inside the house he heard the sounds of his daughter and her boyfriend laughing as though they had been freed of all their senses. Greatly concerned, he walked upstairs and pounded parentally on Gwendolyn's door.

"What's going on in there?" he demanded.

He allowed a few seconds for some sort of answer, but when none came he opened the door. There he found the two of them laughing and rolling on her bed.

"What are you doing?" he shouted.

Drunk as he was, Cedric jumped up and immediately discerned that this was a bad spot to be found in. He had seen enough angry fathers in his time to know when to hasten a retreat.

Without a word to either of them, he ran past Ishmael, who immediately turned around and started to chase after the young man. In his inebriated state, Cedric made a single, critical miscalculation as he reached the bottom of the stairs, a miscalculation that would ensure that he and the older gentleman would spend a lot more time together than either would have wished. Instead of turning left and running out the front door, he turned right and for some inexplicable reason headed down to the cellar. Over the decades, whenever Ishmael grew sour, he would demand that Cedric tell him what in blazes he was thinking going down there. Cedric would always just shrug his shoulders and insist that he didn't know, that it seemed like a good idea at the time.

The cellar stairway was rickety, not the sort of structure wise men ran down. As Cedric sped down its steps, he heard the sound of wood snapping in half. Before he could react, he fell face first towards the stairway, which smashed apart as his body hit it. Ishmael was too enraged to see or hear what was happening and as he followed Cedric down into the cellar he discovered—too late—that the stairway wasn't there anymore.

Cedric died when his head smashed onto the floor, and Ishmael died when he became impaled on a piece of broken wood. Neither of them was too pleased about it.

A sobered Gwendolyn was the first person to come across this scene, and as she sobbed and cried, she vowed never to touch alcohol again. Over the years that followed she became a zealous member of the growing temperance movement and in the 1920s was instrumental in helping to pass the Prohibition Amendment. But before then, in 1905, she sold the house on Winslow and Vine to a pair of newlyweds named the Baxters.

Hugo and Meredith were a sweet and ordinary couple who had bought the large house because its state of ill repair made it the cheapest on the market. Hugo was a carpenter by trade and he slowly fixed the place up, returning it to its former glory. One of the first chores he set for himself was the building of a new staircase to the cellar. This should have been an easy job, but he found his progress greatly inhibited by a series of strange occurrences. His tools seemed to move on their own, as he could never find them in the spots where he remembered placing them. He was unnerved by the sound of laughter that echoed in the dank, dark space. Perhaps laughter was too strong a word, as it more closely resembled a childishly high-pitched giggle of delight. But the thing that made him question the wisdom of finishing the staircase was that shadows moved along the walls. They weren't human, but they also weren't like shadows of any animal he could think of.

When he told Meredith about this, she scolded him for being so foolish. "There's no such thing as ghosts," she insisted.

"But the shadows! The laughter!" Hugo protested.

Meredith shook her head impatiently. "It's just rats," she explained. "I tell you what, tomorrow I'll go to the store and buy you a book on how to get rid of them."

Hugo could see that nothing he could say would convince her, so he decided that he would have to show her instead.

"I'm too busy to spend my time killing rats," he told her. "If you want to get rid of them, then do it yourself."

Meredith rolled her eyes. "Suit yourself," she retorted, "just don't let it get around that you're so easily frightened by a couple of shadows and squeaks."

The next day Meredith made good on her promise and bought a book on rat catching. She read it carefully and then gathered the supplies it suggested and took them, along with the book, down to the cellar.

She was there for just over two minutes before something caused her to drop everything and run back upstairs.

That was how Ishmael got his book.

* * *

Over the years that followed, the Baxters did their best to avoid the cellar. They felt a little more comfortable there when they were able to install electricity in the house and a light bulb illuminated the space. But even then, they went down to the cellar only when they absolutely had to.

In 1948, Hugo had a heart attack and died, leaving Meredith alone in the large house. Her visits to the cellar became even more infrequent, and in 1962, they stopped completely when she passed away in her sleep.

During the years after Hugo's death, the house fell back into disrepair and a city-wide recession left the corner of Winslow and Vine an undesirable place to live. After Meredith died, the house remained vacant for close to 40 years. But in 2003, the neighborhood underwent a metamorphosis, thanks to a resurgence in the city's economy and a determined effort to beautify its slums. A young professional couple named the Batemans bought the house on the corner.

Even though their purchase was going to cost them thousands of dollars in repairs and restoration, Nathan and Brittany were excited to own a house that was unique and part of the city's history. The place was still too run-down to live in, so they stayed in a nearby hotel while they commuted between their jobs and their new investment, where they did a lot of the work themselves. They had owned the house for two weeks when Nathan, who was a lawyer, thought he heard a strange clinking noise coming from the cellar.

"Do you hear that?" he asked Brittany.

"What?"

"Listen…"

"I don't hear anything."

"Can't you hear it? It sounds like someone hitting a pipe with a wrench or something."

"I don't hear it."

"I'll go check it out."

"You do that."

"Did you put any new light bulbs down there?"

"I thought you did."

"Why would you think that?"

"Because you said you were going to."

"When?"

"Yesterday."

"No, I didn't. Did I?"

"Yep."

"I guess I'll do it now, while I check down there. Where did you put the new bulbs?"

"They're in the plastic bag by the front door."

"Thanks."

Nathan went over and grabbed a couple of light bulbs and then walked over to the cellar door. He opened it and stuck his head into the darkness.

"That's strange," he said to Brittany, who was standing behind him. "Now I don't hear it."

* * *

Ishmael and Cedric were both so shocked by Nathan's sudden appearance that they froze in place and watched him as he screwed a new light bulb into the ancient socket. When he was finished he turned the light on and walked down into the cellar to check it out. Ishmael looked over to Cedric to see what he would do. The younger ghost had spent the last few decades pining for someone to come down the stairs, but now that his wish had come true he had no idea what to do. All the years he had spent planning and devising new tricks and games proved worthless when his moment of truth arrived. All he could do was watch as the new homeowner walked around.

Brittany stuck her head through the door.

"Anything down there?" she asked.

"Yeah," Nathan answered, "but it's all under 10 pounds of dust."

"Want me to bring down the vacuum?"

"Please."

As Brittany went off to get the appliance, Nathan spotted something unusual on a dusty old chair. He picked it up and looked at it.

"What's that you've got there?" Brittany asked as she carried down the vacuum.

"A book," Nathan answered.

"A book? Down here?"

"Yeah," he chuckled, "and guess what it's called."

"I don't know."

"*Catching Rats and Other Vermin: A Homeowner's Guide.* This thing has got to be a hundred years old."

"How'd it get down here?"

"Beats me."

Ishmael was red with anger.

"They took my book!" he ranted. "Those interlopers came here and stole my book!"

"It's not that bad," Cedric said, trying to calm him down. "It's not like you haven't read it a million billion times. Plus they did clean the place up. You've been whining about that for years now."

"That's not the point! The book was mine and they stole it! It was all I had! For close to a century the only thing keeping me sane was that book, and now it's gone!"

"I think you're making a big deal about nothing," Cedric decided. "I'm excited. It'll be good to have new people to play with again."

"That's all you think about, isn't it? Yourself! Of course you're happy, you've been waiting for this ever since the old lady died!"

"Ishmael!" Cedric shouted uncharacteristically. "It was just a book. And for all you know they might end up building a library down here."

Ishmael snorted derisively.

"No one in their right mind would use a damp cellar like this as a library."

"Then what do you think they are going to use it for?"

Before Ishmael could answer, Nathan opened the door, turned on the light and started walking down the stairs. A short man carrying a pencil and a writing pad followed him. Nathan spoke to the man as they walked down.

"As soon as I came down here I knew it would serve as a perfect wine cellar," he explained to the man. He then described in detail how he wanted the shelving to be built and where it was all to go. Five minutes later they were back upstairs.

The surge of elation that coursed through Cedric's veins was so pure and powerful it nearly paralyzed him. He still could not believe his ears.

"Did you hear what he said?" he asked Ishmael, who didn't answer him. "A WINE CELLAR!" Suddenly he was able to move again and to prove it he danced and jumped around, while his cellarmate just sat in a corner and fumed.

"If they think they are building anything down here, they are sadly mistaken," the bitter older ghost declared.

This caused Cedric to stop mid-jig.

"What do you mean?"

"I mean exactly what I said. Nothing is going to be built down here as long as I don't have my book."

"But you can't do that!"

"Oh, no? Watch me!"

Absolutely nothing happened for several days after that. The two ghosts listened as the sounds of power tools hummed, screeched, thumped and whirred up above. Cedric was hoping that during this time Ishmael would find a way to calm down, but as the days passed his cellarmate only got angrier as he imagined what sorts of changes this new couple were inflicting on what had once been his house.

"Can you imagine what those philistines are doing to my lovely home? Listen! You can hear them dismantle it as I speak!"

As if to punctuate this sentiment, something crashed loudly to the floor upstairs.

"You don't know what they're doing," Cedric insisted, "and you never got mad when the other people who lived here made changes to the house."

"Because they were civilized!" Ishmael answered back. "I knew I could trust them. I *cannot* trust these people! They're book stealers!"

"Will you get over that already," Cedric sighed.

"Never!"

Just then the cellar door opened. A group of men walked down the stairs carrying toolboxes and other equipment. Cedric could see an almost insane look build in Ishmael's eyes, and before the older ghost could do anything to the workers Cedric jumped on him.

"What are you doing?" Ishmael shouted angrily at his tackler.

"I'm keeping you from doing something stupid," answered Cedric.

"Get off me, you big oaf!"

"Not until these nice gentlemen are finished."

Ishmael swore at Cedric and struggled underneath him, but the younger ghost proved to be too strong to escape from. Out of frustration, Ishmael kicked his left foot into the air and—to his satisfaction—it hit the behind of one of the laborers.

"Owwww! What the hell was that?" shouted the man as he felt the blow.

"What's the matter with you?" asked his boss.

"Something just kicked me," complained the man as he rubbed his sore behind.

His boss shook his head with exasperation. "What'd I tell you about drinking on the job?" he sighed.

The man started to protest that he was sober, then remembered the two beers he had drunk during lunch. With a frown on his face, he got to work.

Cedric dragged Ishmael out of foot's reach of the workers and sat on him as the men spent the rest of the day building shelves for the Batemans' wine collection. Ishmael cursed him the entire time and promised that his revenge would be slow and sweet. The project didn't take the men long and when they finished and left, Cedric stood up and helped Ishmael to his feet.

"I suppose you're going to smash everything up now, huh?" Cedric asked him.

"No," Ishmael said coolly. "I have decided that that is not the best action to take at this moment."

"What are you going to do?"

For the first time since the two of them had died, Ishmael allowed himself a smile.

"Wouldn't you like to know?" he answered.

Three long weeks passed during which nothing happened. Cedric and Ishmael listened as the sounds of work above them slowly began to peter out, until finally, one day, there was silence. This lasted for two days, until the sounds of people moving in could be heard.

"I guess it's official now, huh?" Cedric said to Ishmael, who stayed quiet.

Up above them furniture screeched as it was pushed across the floor. The sounds of breaking glass echoed as the careless movers dropped boxes that were marked fragile. Nathan and Brittany could be heard arguing about what was supposed to go where and about who had hired the incompetent movers.

Cedric waited impatiently for someone to come downstairs with a few bottles of wine to fit into the new shelving. He hoped they had enough that it would be hard for them to keep track if one or two went missing. He had no idea if he was even capable of drinking any, but the thought of opening a bottle and smelling it seemed most appealing. Ishmael, on the other hand, just sat in a corner and stayed quiet in a way that Cedric found uncomfortably sinister.

It took three long days, but finally Cedric was rewarded when the young Batemans walked down into their wine cellar with several boxes full of bottles of very good wine. He watched rapturously as they argued over what kind of system they should organize the bottles in. Brittany wanted to organize them alphabetically and by type, while Nathan insisted that the only rational way to organize the bottles was chronologically and by type. Eventually they decided to compromise, with Nathan organizing the red wines and Brittany the whites. Cedric didn't care how they were organized; he just wanted them to go so he could open a bottle. He couldn't believe how many there were. He had been in saloons that weren't as well stocked as this. Finally the bickering couple got them all put away and went back upstairs. As soon as they were gone, he ran to the bottles and grabbed one at random. It was a merlot, and he looked at it admiringly and noticed with a sense of awe that it had been bottled the same year the two of them had died. Not having a corkscrew, the best he could do to open it was smash the neck against the wall. The sound was loud enough for him to worry that they might come downstairs to investigate, but nothing happened so after a minute he tried to drink it. The red liquid splashed against the ground, but to his giddy delight he found he could still taste it.

"It's even better than I remembered," he laughed to Ishmael before offering him the bottle. "Do you want some?"

"No," Ishmael answered coldly.

Cedric was too happy to let Ishmael's bad attitude drag him down. He let the whole bottle splash to the floor and in his ghostly drunkenness sang a song he remembered from his carousing days about a young lady of easy virtue.

Even as a ghost, Cedric could not hold his liquor. Just a few hours after his first bottle of wine in a century, he was on the floor of the cellar, snoring loudly and oblivious to the world. Ishmael looked out the one small window that was their only outlet to the outside world and waited for the night sky to fall and the moon to rise. When it did he calmly walked over to the shelves of wine and grabbed a bottle and smashed it hard against the floor. A rush of pure joy came over him and he started to smash more bottles, row by row.

With a sudden start Cedric woke up and saw what Ishmael was doing. He was horrified by what he saw but was still too incapacitated to do anything about it.

"Stop it!" he shouted at Ishmael. "They're going to hear you!"

Ishmael apparently didn't care as he continued to smash bottle after bottle.

Cedric was soon proved right. The cellar door burst open and the light went on. The Batemans ran downstairs in their underwear and were treated to the sight of their beloved and expensive bottles of wine being lifted out of their individual cubbies and smashed to the ground by a strange invisible force. By now the ground was far too littered with broken glass for them to approach the phantom in their midst, so all they could do was watch as it destroyed every last bottle that they had.

They stood awestruck. It took a long time for one of them to speak.

"Did you see that?" asked Nathan.

"Uh-huh," his wife answered.

"Do you think it was what I think it was?"

"That depends on what you thought it was."

"I don't want to say."

"Neither do I."

"Because that would be crazy."

"Insane."

"And we're not crazy or insane."

"Nope."

"We should call someone."

"Like who?"

"Don't you know that woman? The crazy one?"

"Yeah. She'd be perfect for this."

* * *

Zandra was positive.

"Oh, yeah," she told them, "you've got ghosts all right. Two of them. A young guy and an older fella. The young guy's kinda sweet and seems to like you two, while the other guy is a real pain in the you-know-where. He wants his book back."

"Book?" asked Nathan.

"Apparently there was a book down there that you brought back up with you. He kinda grew attached to it over the years and would like to have it back."

"Is he the one who destroyed our wine collection?" asked Brittany.

"Yep, and he's just gonna get worse until you get him his book back."

"And you say the other one is friendly?" asked Nathan.

"Seemed to be. Although I don't think he's that bright, to be honest with you. And I think he's a bit of a souse."

Nathan and Brittany looked at each other for a moment, before Brittany turned back to Zandra.

"So, this older ghost likes to read, huh?"

* * *

Later that same day the cellar door opened and Nathan walked in. He walked cautiously down the steps, afraid of having a run-in with Ishmael who was in fact standing in the corner farthest away from him. In his arms Nathan carried a large heavy box. He brought it down to the cellar floor and dropped it with a heavy thud.

"Sorry about that," he apologized to the air before he turned around and went back up.

"What's that?" Cedric said as he approached the box after Nathan was gone.

"I certainly don't care," sniffed Ishmael.

Curious, Cedric opened the box and smiled.

"I really think you're going to like this."

"Why? What is it?"

"Just get over here and take a look."

Skeptically Ishmael strode over to the box and looked inside. For the first time since he had died, tears came to his eyes.

"There's so many of them," he whispered as he looked at all the different books.

"And I think this is for me," Cedric smiled when he spotted a small bottle of whiskey between two hardcovers. "I think I could get used to this," he smiled.

"Me too," Ishmael grinned. "Me too."

From that point on Brittany and Nathan kept their two ghosts neck deep in books and booze, which made Cedric and Ishmael so happy they didn't mind the tour groups and camera crews that the enterprising young couple brought down to the cellar to share in the miracle of their haunted home. Eventually this enterprise became so lucrative that the two of them were able to quit their jobs and devote themselves full time to a tour service that led people all around Braggsville's various spooky sites. They also set up several web cameras inside the cellar and charged people $14.95 a month to watch as Cedric and Ishmael did what ghosts do. Cedric loved all this new attention and although he never really understood what the cameras were for, he still was able to figure out that he should provide some sort of show as long as they were there. Ishmael ignored everyone and just kept himself happy reading his books. And now that he had so many to choose from, he refused to touch any that even mentioned the subject of rats.

Mary's Tree

Mary's Tree was certainly a sight to behold. It was huge and black and dead—with a strangely polished sheen that made it look as though some insane undertaker had taken a dozen gnarled and deformed caskets and stacked them up lengthwise end to end. Its branches were barren of any life—no bird dared to nest on its limbs—and the way they hung suggested that they could lunge at you with an almost calculated menace, snatch you away and send you down to the hell that was home to its long and tangled roots. Mr. Lomax had wanted to cut it down ever since he bought Billingsgate Castle five years before, but no matter how much money he offered to the people of the community, no one dared take it. The story of that tree was one of Billingsgate's oldest legends, and no one wanted to be responsible for what would happen when it was cut down.

In the end, Mr. Lomax had to look outside the community to find someone willing to take down Mary's Tree. From a friend he got the number of a handyman and contractor named Ben Simpson, who lived three counties away in the small town of Tisdale. At first, Ben was taken aback by Mr. Lomax's request. The job seemed too simple to call a man who lived almost 500 miles away, but his misgivings vanished when Mr. Lomax offered to quadruple his usual fee and pay all his travel expenses. Ben told the man that he would be there by the end of the week.

When Ben and his son, Kim, drove onto the Lomax property three days later, they were both shocked by the century-and-a-half-old building that sat on it. They had heard of the infamous Billingsgate Castle (or Billy's Folly, as it was also known), but neither had dreamed that the tree they had traveled so far to cut would be found on its front lawn. The history of the castle was the stuff of urban legend, full of tales passed around by children in front of campfires as they roasted marshmallows and fought the urge to sleep.

One hundred sixty-two years before, a man named William Billingsgate had built the castle in honor of his new bride. Only 27, William had inherited his fortune from his father, who had gotten rich in the slave trade. A kind, sensitive young man, William was disgusted that his comfort was the result of so much suffering, so he made it his life's work to become one of the era's most charitable philanthropists. Hundreds of trusts and organizations, as well as schools and hospitals, were founded in his name, but most of his efforts focused on his dream of building a perfect community. To that end he purchased 10,000 acres of land and started to build on it. His belief that people would flock to his new city once they heard about it turned out to be right. As people arrived from all corners of the world, he tried to christen his community New Eden, but its new citizens feared that such a name might be considered blasphemous and started calling it Billingsgate among themselves. Despite William's protests, the name stuck.

An obviously romantic soul, William was fascinated by the legends of King Arthur and the Knights of Camelot. In his daydreams he often imagined himself as a benevolent king who ruled over his subjects with a practical wisdom that kept him from becoming despotic. He also dreamed of finding a queen worthy to share his kingdom with him, so as Billingsgate's population grew, he looked to it to find himself a wife.

There were many beautiful women in the town, and if William's search had focused on looks alone, he would have had many women to choose from. But William was not searching for a beauty, he was searching for a queen, and in Billingsgate that left him with only one prospect.

Her name was Mary. The daughter of Angus and Morag Deayton, she worked as a waitress in her parents' restaurant, where she dazzled customers with her style and grace. Her hair was as dark as obsidian, and it hung in soft almost-curls all the way down her back. Her voice was soft and quiet, but it carried with it a weight that held others' ears and forced them to listen. She was small, barely 5' 1", but her shape and bearing were such that people assumed she was at least half a foot taller. While these qualities alone would not be enough to make her stand out in a place as ridiculously endowed as Billingsgate, what set her apart were her eyes. They were the darkest and deepest possible violet and they looked out into the world with a stare so confident the sun itself would have trouble arguing if she ordered it not to rise.

The first time he saw her, William knew she was the one. With her father's enthusiastic approval he began to court her, and then only three months later he asked her to be his wife. If he was offended by her request to allow her to think about it, he did not show it.

Mary knew very well the type of life she could have as William's wife, but she wasn't sure if she was willing to marry a man she didn't love just to ensure herself a lifetime of comfort. In the end, it was only the thought of what the marriage could do for her parents that persuaded her to say yes.

The wedding was lavish, with everyone from Billingsgate invited. During the celebration William stood and told the townspeople that he had decided to tear down the mansion he lived in at the center of town and replace it with a home more worthy of his beautiful bride.

"My queen deserves a castle!" he shouted to his guests, most of whom assumed he was joking.

Mr. Lomax walked out the castle's front door to greet Ben and Kim. A huge smile lit up his face as he shook their hands.

"I can't tell you how long I've wanted to get rid of this thing!" he laughed.

Ben and Kim looked up and studied the tree, which looked nothing like any they had encountered before.

"Was this tree ever set on fire?" Kim asked Mr. Lomax, unused to seeing a tree so unnaturally black.

Their employer hesitated before answering. "I don't think so."

It was obvious to Ben and Kim that he had another answer but didn't want to share it.

As big and dangerous as the tree looked, Ben and Kim decided that cutting it down wouldn't be anything out of the ordinary, so they went back to their truck and took out everything they needed. As they started setting up, a group of children gathered about 50 feet behind them. It wasn't unusual for kids to want to watch them work, so the two of them smiled and waved at the kids, who just stared back at them with inscrutable looks on their young faces. Soon other people arrived and stood with the children. Men and women of all ages gathered to watch Ben and Kim cut down the tree, and their presence made the two men uncomfortable. After 15 minutes, close to 50 people were there. They did not speak or even make a sound but just stood and watched. It was clear that they expected to see something, and Ben and Kim couldn't help wondering what it was.

In an age when $20,000 could build a home so large and exquisite people would travel from miles around just to say they saw it, William had spent nearly half a million dollars on his tribute to his new wife. It was designed to look like a real European castle, and no expense had been spared in its creation. On several occasions whole parts of it had to be rebuilt because they did not precisely meet William's expectations. He was so enthralled by the project that he failed to notice how uninterested his wife was in it. She had never asked for a castle and didn't care if she ever lived in one. She was too kind to tell him so, but she would have been a lot happier just living in his old house.

After two long years Billingsgate Castle was finally completed. William filled it with expensive European art and furniture that he had commissioned from the continent's finest craftsmen. For their bedroom he himself designed a large canopy bed with cameos of his and Mary's profiles embedded in the headboard.

Mary did her best to look excited as he showed her around their new home, but she felt little joy. The castle was cold and dark and not even the finest decorations could warm it up. To her the place felt closer to a prison than a home.

Ben walked over to Mr. Lomax.

"Do you have any idea what's going on here?" he asked, referring to their ever-growing audience.

Mr. Lomax shrugged nervously and shook his head.

"Fine, you don't have to tell me," Ben told him, "but if you don't, me and my son are going to go home and you can keep your tree."

"I'll double what I'm paying you," Mr. Lomax offered, trying to avoid an explanation.

Ben thought about this. Doubling what they were being paid now would mean that they would be paid eight times what they usually charged. For that kind of money, he was willing to deal with a little mystery. He went back to work.

After a year living in the castle with her husband, Mary was afraid that she would go insane. Her parents had taken ill and died, and she found herself alone in the castle. It was so quiet, while at the same time it echoed with tiny unexplainable noises that made her skin crawl. No matter how many candles or lamps they lit, it was always too dark for her liking, even during the daytime. Worst of all, though, was the effect it was having on William.

Living in the castle allowed him to succumb to the allure of his fantasies. The more time he spent there, the more he came to believe that he actually was a king. Soon everyone in the castle was required to address him as "Your Highness" and treat him as though he actually was some kind of monarch. He called his wife Queen Mary and insisted on going on "quests" to prove his love to her. Mary found it almost impossible to tolerate this lunacy, but she had no way to escape it. As crazy as William had become, he was still the most powerful man around and could easily destroy her and everyone she cared about if she tried to leave him. The thought of this overtook her with despair, and her only comfort came from her daily ride. The hour she spent each day on her horse was the only time she felt free, and she came to depend on it as if it were a life-saving drug.

It was because of this dependency that she came to the attention of a handsome young man who had been hired to work in the stable. His name was Christopher and he had a strong chin and bright blue eyes. He took special care of Iris, Mary's favorite horse, and was feeding the animal some oats when its owner appeared behind him.

"You're very gentle with her," Mary said to him.

"Yes, ma'am," he nodded.

"It is rare for a strong man to be able to be that gentle."

"So you say, ma'am."

While the two of them never directly expressed it, it was clear that they were attracted to each other. Before and after Mary's daily ride, they always managed to talk to each other. Even though their discussions were always innocent, others around them began to gossip about their relationship. Although Mary had never been unfaithful to William, many people assumed that she and Christopher were lovers.

It was only a matter of time before this rumor made its way to William. His reaction proved terrifying. With the anger of a once-just king driven mad by the ingratitude of his subjects, he had his wife and Christopher brought before him. Both insisted that the rumor was a lie and that their friendship was purely innocent. William, however, needed only one look at Christopher's handsome face to become convinced that his queen had cuckolded him.

"You are traitors to this kingdom," he coldly explained to them, "and the penalty for treason is death."

Mary wept and Christopher struggled as they were both dragged outside. Two ropes were hung from the limbs of a large elm tree that was surrounded by several torches. Both of them were placed on top of horses, Mary onto Iris and Christopher onto an old mare that could barely support his weight. Nooses were slipped around their necks, and the two of them waited while William walked out of the castle and stood in front of them, a lit torch in his hand eerily illuminating his face.

"I am sorry it has come to this," he insisted. He turned his head to the man who held the reins of the horse Christopher sat on and nodded. The man let go of the reins, shouted and slapped the mare on its flank. The horse moved slowly, and it took several seconds before the rope around Christopher's neck jerked tightly. His body swung off the horse, where it struggled against the terror of asphyxiation. Mary watched in horror as it took several long and agonizing moments for her friend to die. When, at last, Christopher's life finally ended, William turned to his beautiful wife and spoke to her.

"See what you have done? You have made me kill a man. I want this on your conscience as we live out the rest of our days."

Mary realized then that the noose around her neck was merely meant to scare her and that William had no intention of hanging her. She stopped crying. It was clear to her what she had to do.

Just as the man who held Iris' reins let go of them so he could remove the noose from around Mary's neck, Mary shouted "Faster, Iris!" and kicked her heels into the horse's flanks. Iris listened to her owner and ran as fast as she could. The noose tightened around Mary's throat and snapped her neck in two.

William screamed when he saw his wife hang at the end of the rope he had ordered placed around her neck.

"This is your fault!" he shouted at Christopher's lifeless body where it still hung from the tree. He then ran to the swinging corpse and set it aflame with his torch. His servants tried to stop the fire, fearing it would spread, but William ordered them to stop. "Let it all burn," he commanded. "Let it all burn."

Before the tree could be turned to ash, a hard rain began to fall. It put out the fire and left a blackened tree and the charred remains of two friends. William refused to deal with the matter any further, so the servants decided to bury what was left of Mary and Christopher at the foot of the damaged tree. They couldn't explain why it felt appropriate, but they all agreed that it did.

As the months passed, it became evident that those involved in what happened on that horrible night would not go unpunished for their crimes. Almost immediately William took ill with a pain in his stomach. He began to cough up blood and soon went blind. His flesh began to itch and burn to such a degree that he could not stop screaming. The suddenness and the ferocity with which his symptoms appeared confused and vexed every doctor available. They tried every cure and remedy they could think of, but nothing worked. As he suffered, the servants who helped him that night began to die in strange accidents that defied explanation. One was found at the bottom of a well, missing his head, and another was found burned to death in the middle of a field. Before the year was through, only William remained alive, although in his case this was not a blessing but a curse. For 10 long and agonizing years he suffered from his mysterious illness, dying only when a nurse, unable to take his screams a moment longer, fed him some food laced with arsenic.

During the years that he suffered, the burned tree that was a constant reminder of his crime managed to somehow grow and become stronger, although it was dead. The people of Billingsgate came to believe that Mary's spirit lived inside it and was the avenging force that took all those lives. They vowed never to cut it down for fear that Mary's wrath might be visited upon them.

After William died the castle remained empty off and on throughout the decades, its various owners never keeping the property very long. Of them all, the most recent owner had managed to stay the longest.

Mr. Lomax tapped his foot impatiently as he waited for Ben and Kim to get to work. He couldn't wait to rid himself of this travesty of nature. He stood away from the crowd, members of which would occasionally throw him dirty looks. He did his best to ignore them.

Ben started up his chainsaw and placed its blade against the trunk of the tree. As it cut through the wood, Ben noticed that some sort of strange red syrup was leaking from the cut. He turned off his chainsaw and took off one of his gloves. He dipped a finger into the syrup and lifted it up to his face to inspect it.

"What is it?" his son asked him.

Ben spoke under his breath. "It's blood."

"Is there a bat or something in there?"

"Yeah," Ben nodded, but he sounded unconvinced. He slipped his glove back on, restarted his chainsaw and went back to work. As he cut deeper and deeper, a sound began to fight against the roar of his equipment.

It was the sound of a woman crying.

Ben turned off his chainsaw once again. Its blade was soaked with blood.

"Do you hear that?" he asked Kim.

Kim nodded.

They turned around to look at the crowd to see if what they were doing was causing someone to cry, but the crowd was as stoic as ever and the sound of the crying was definitely coming from the tree.

Then, among the tears, a woman's voice could be heard.

"Don't stop," the voice pleaded. "Please, don't stop."

Ben and his son looked at each other. They had heard the same thing. As scared as they were, the depth of emotion in the spirit's voice moved them both.

Kim spoke first. His voice had to fight its way past the knot that was lodged in his throat.

"You heard her," he told his father. "Get back to work."

Ben nodded and started up his chainsaw one last time.

By the end of the day, beyond the patch of dirt that was surrounded by green grass, there was no evidence that the tree had ever existed. Mr. Lomax wrote out a check to the two men, but Ben refused to accept it.

"I don't understand what happened here today," he explained, "but I think it was something that should've happened a long time ago, and I'm just happy knowing that I was the man who did it."

Ben and his son drove home. They never told anyone back in Tisdale about what they had experienced on that strange day in Billingsgate, but for the rest of their lives they felt as if they had been blessed. They never said it aloud, but they could both feel the presence of another person's gratitude, and the desire that the debt owed them be repaid. They both felt that they weren't owed anything, but Mary disagreed.

The Charitable Spirit

Neil sighed and stretched his arms above his head as the automatic dialer he was connected to waited for a person to pick up the phone. Sometimes the person answered as soon as the last call ended, and sometimes it took several minutes. This randomness was just one of the many things he had come to despise about his job as a telemarketer.

"Hello?" he heard an older-sounding woman answer. The tone of her voice indicated that she was surprised to have someone call her at this time of day.

He looked at the name that had just come up on his computer.

"Hello, is this Rebecca Dumont I'm talking to?"

"Yeah…"

"Hi, Ms. Dumont, my name is Neil and I'm calling on behalf of the National Association for Visually Impaired Athletes."

"The what?"

"It's an association dedicated to the idea that just because a person has a vision-related disability that's no reason for them to be denied the great personal satisfaction that comes from athletic achievement. We here at N.A.V.I.A. do our best to fund blind and legally blind athletes as they train for such international events as the Paralympics, which I'm sure you've heard—"

"What do you want?"

"Well, as I'm sure you understand, a foundation such as ours requires support from the community and so we're calling you in the hopes that you'd be willing to generously contribute a tax-deductible donation of $15 or more—"

"Look, I don't have any money and if I did I wouldn't give it to you. Nobody does anything to help me out, so I don't see why I should do anything for anybody else."

Neil rolled his eyes at this, but he managed to remain polite. "Well, I'm sorry for bothering you, ma'am, and I hope you have a pleasant night."

She hung up.

"Nice attitude, lady," he muttered as the dialer went searching for a new household. Surprisingly, though, he had found that this sort of response was actually pretty rare. When he started the job he had expected that most people would act rudely towards his intrusion into their lives, but the truth was that most people—even the ones with no intention of donating money to a telephone solicitor—treated him with nothing but respect and kindness. As nice as this was to find out, it didn't make the job any less agonizing. Since starting three days before, he had talked to 669 strangers. In that time he had managed to convince 13 of them to donate money to the charity he was calling for, which meant that he had been told "no" by 656 different people. It would be a blow to any person's ego.

At this point on his third day, he had been on the phone for two hours and 40 minutes and had managed to collect a total of $15 from an elderly East Indian man who Neil was pretty certain had no idea what Neil was talking about. As each successive call after that ended in failure, a gnawing sensation of fear started growing in the pit of his stomach. His rent was late and his fridge was empty, and this job was the only one he could find. If he didn't start meeting his daily quota by the end of the week, there was a good chance he would have to move back in with his parents. He really didn't want to have to do that, so as the dialer took its time finding him someone new to talk to, he tried to convince himself that this time he was going to make it happen.

"Hello?" he heard a young woman answer. That was good—8 of the 13 people he had been able to get money from had been young women.

He looked at the computer in front of him. On it he saw the young woman's name, address and telephone number.

"Hello, is this Tamra Mueler I'm talking to?" He tried his best to sound suave.

"Yes it is, and who is this?" She sounded sweet and friendly, like someone who dealt with young children as part of her job.

"Hi, Tamra, my name is Neil—"

"Hi, Neil," she interrupted politely.

"Hi," he repeated as he tried to stay on track with his spiel. "I'm calling you on behalf of the National Association for Visually Impaired Athletes."

"You mean N.A.V.I.A.?"

"That's right! Have you heard of our association?" Almost nobody he had talked to had.

"Oh, of course! My older brother Joss won the silver medal in the 100-meter sprint at the last Paralympics."

"Is he blind?"

"He was. He died in a car accident six months ago."

Neil hated it when people shared information like this with him.

"I'm so sorry," he said sympathetically.

"That's okay, you had nothing to do with it."

"Still, it's horrible when things like that happen to a family."

"Truth be told, Neil, we Muelers kind of get used to it. We're a pretty accident-prone bunch. I figure we average two or three funerals a year. Luckily there's a lot of us still around, so we aren't going to run out any time soon."

Neil was surprised by how chipper and upbeat she sounded about her family's penchant for tragedy, but her attitude made him smile.

"So," she continued, "I bet you guys are running your annual pledge drive right now, huh?"

"That's right."

"Well, you are in luck, because I just sold a bunch of Joss' stuff and I bet he'd want the money to go to you guys. How does $600 sound?"

"Uh..." Neil was rendered speechless by his good fortune. Just when things were beginning to look bleak, this wonderful angel named Tamra came along and made a donation that was double his daily quota. And he didn't even have to give her his spiel!

"You still there, Neil?" Tamra said, laughing.

"Yes!" Neil regained his composure and decided to close this call as soon as possible before she decided to change her mind. "I just need to confirm the information I have here." He then asked her for the correct way to spell her name and her current address and telephone number. Everything matched up with what was on his screen and he threw up his hand to get the attention of his supervisor. "Now, Tamra, I'm just going to have you talk to one of my superiors for a second and he's going to confirm the amount of your donation." He then slipped off his headset and handed it to the heavy-set man who had just appeared at his side. The large man bent down to look at the computer screen.

"Hello, is this Tamra I'm talking to?"

Neil smiled proudly as his supervisor, who had given him a lecture about trying harder just half an hour before, confirmed Tamra's very generous donation.

"Well, thank you very much for your support, Tamra." With that said the supervisor took off the headset and handed it back to Neil. "Good job, kid!" He patted Neil on the back.

"Thanks." Neil smiled.

"A few more like that and you're looking at a promotion." The large man grinned before he turned and walked away.

Neil turned back towards his computer and saw that it had gone blank. That meant it was break time, so with a burst of energy he stood up and walked over to the lunchroom. It was all he could do to stop himself from whistling, he was so happy.

He grabbed an orange from the fridge, sat down at one of the tables and directed his attention to the large television in the corner. The news was on. He started peeling his orange as one of the news anchors described a bizarre incident that had been uncovered earlier in the day.

"—because of complaints from neighbors about the smell that was coming from the apartment."

The camera then cut to a middle-aged policeman who, in a segment taped earlier in the day, explained what they had found.

"The best we can determine at this time is that sometime earlier in the month the young woman tripped and fell and hit her head on her coffee table and died from her injuries. From the information that we have gathered she was packing to go on a vacation to Hawaii, and that's why no one she knew became suspicious by her absence. As far as they were concerned she wasn't due back until next week."

A picture of an attractive blonde woman in her mid-20s replaced the policeman on the TV screen and was accompanied by a voiceover from the news anchor.

"Tamra Mueler was 26 and worked full time at the Happy Tot Day Care Center. She is survived by her parents and seven siblings."

Neil dropped his half-peeled orange on the floor as he tried to figure out how many Tamra Muelers there could be in the city.

A tearful woman who looked like an older version of Tamra replaced the photograph on the television screen. According to the caption, she was Tamra's mother.

"It just hurts so much," she explained, "because we were just getting over the death of our son Joss..."

The blood in Neil's body began to rush to his head. He didn't know what was freaking him out more, the fact that he had just talked to a ghost or that there was no way for Tamra to make good on her pledge. Somehow he managed to stand and walk back to his cubicle, where he grabbed his jacket and picked up his backpack. He put them on, then walked over to his supervisor and told him that he was quitting and asked when he could pick up his paycheck.

His supervisor seemed stunned by this news. "But you just hit the jackpot! You're on a roll! Why would you want to quit now?"

"Dude," Neil sighed, "as much as I hate the idea of moving back in with my parents, there's no way it could be worse than asking for money from the dead." Before his supervisor could make any sense out of this pearl of wisdom, Neil turned around and walked out the office's door.

He didn't talk to people on the phone much after that.

Loyalty

The parking lot was dark, as usual. The maintenance people were always slow to replace its burned-out light bulbs, and as a result there was a whole valley of darkness in the middle in which an entire gang of murderous psychopaths could easily hide. Usually Donna would ask one of her strapping young coworkers to escort her to her car when she left for the day, but tonight she had had to stay late and finish working on an important brief that was due in the morning. By the time she was finished she was the only person in the building, save for Artie, the near-senile security guard whom she had found sleeping at his station. She decided to let him sleep and brave the dark underground structure by herself, but she grabbed her pepper spray from her purse as she rode down the elevator. A minute later its doors opened and with her aerosol weapon clutched tightly in her right hand, Donna took a deep breath and stepped out into the dark and eerily silent structure.

She walked quickly, cursing herself for parking at the other end of the lot. Her footsteps echoed like gunshots throughout the space, loud enough to wake any maniac who might have fallen asleep while waiting for her to appear. She kept her head up and tried to look confident and ready to defend herself as she made her way down the long expanse of concrete, but as she got closer to her car her stylish heel stepped on a small stone and she lost her balance. Her ankle twisted painfully and she fell to the ground with a graceless thud. The momentum caused her to drop her pepper spray and it slid underneath her car. Her ankle burned with pain, but the absurdity of her fall was enough to make her laugh out loud. Gingerly, she tried to stand and immediately discovered that she couldn't put any weight on her right leg. With a sigh, she sat down on the parking lot's floor, took off her shoes and hopped on her left leg to her car. When she got there, she rummaged in her purse for her keys and opened her door. She slumped into her seat, and realized that she had never once driven a car using her left foot and had no idea if it was even possible for her to do it now.

Before she could find out, a dark hand grabbed her from behind. She screamed, but not for long. Once again, the parking lot became eerily silent, save for the almost imperceptible sound of bare feet on concrete.

It was 6:53 AM and Detective Garrison had yet to have a much-needed cup of coffee. With a grim look on his face, he took notes as he and the CSI guy looked over the crime scene.

"What do you figure?" he asked Jenson, the burly forensics expert.

"It looks pretty cut and dried," Jenson shrugged. "The perp broke the passenger side window, got in and waited for her. It doesn't look like she struggled much, but then that doesn't explain why her shoes weren't on her feet and why her pepper spray was under the car, so I'm not sure just yet what happened exactly. We'll know more after the autopsy."

Garrison nodded. The woman's body was already on its way to the morgue. He was about to ask Jenson another question when a young uniformed officer interrupted him.

"People are starting to come in to work. Should we let them in?"

Garrison looked over to Jenson with a raised eyebrow.

"We've already found everything we're going to find," the expert informed him. "You can let them in if you want."

Garrison turned to the kid and nodded silently. Within minutes the empty lot began to fill up with expensive-looking cars.

"Lawyers," he muttered under his breath as a sixth BMW drove into the lot.

Garrison didn't have to go far to continue his investigation. All he had to do was get into the elevator and get out on the fifth floor, which contained the offices of Lynden, Hunter and Associates, the law firm at which the victim, Donna Wendt, had worked. There he spent the next four hours interviewing everyone who worked with her. It soon became clear that Donna was not a well-liked woman. While her coworkers were all shocked by her murder, none of them seemed too disturbed by it. Her secretary, a mousy young woman named Eileen, summed up the reason for this.

"She was a mean, horrible woman," Eileen explained. "I'd call her the b-word, but my mother raised me better than that. Ms. Wendt thought about no one but herself and she made no effort to show anyone the slightest bit of kindness. I don't think I ever heard her say anything nice about anyone."

"Yeah," Garrison nodded, "but did anyone hate her enough to kill her?"

Eileen thought about this for a moment before she answered. "Only about three-quarters of the people in her Rolodex."

Garrison decided to try another line of questioning. "Was she dating anybody?"

"Yeah, a bunch of guys," Eileen told him, "but she was most serious about a guy named Joshua Maynard."

"Another lawyer?"

"No, he's an executive at Rogers and Coombs Advertising. They spent a fair bit of time together."

"He the jealous type?"

"I don't know. The only real contact I've had with him was when he called her to make dinner plans. He sounded pretty normal to me."

"Thanks."

"Don't mention it."

Garrison sat himself down in one of the chairs in front of the modern white desk that took up almost all of Maynard's office space and began to go through the notes he had taken at the law office. He did this for 10 minutes before a handsome man in his mid-30s walked in and introduced himself.

"Hello, Detective," the man said, extending his hand for Garrison to shake. "I'm Joshua Maynard. Sorry to keep you waiting, but I was in a meeting."

"Don't worry about it," said Garrison as Maynard sat down in his chair behind the desk. "Do you know why I'm here?"

"My secretary said it had something to do with Donna, but she wasn't specific. What happened? Did she cheat some old millionaire out of his life savings?"

"No," Garrison answered coldly, annoyed by Maynard's flippancy. "She was found dead this morning. Someone murdered her inside her building's parking lot."

Over the years, Garrison had seen hundreds of people react to the news that someone they knew had been killed, so he considered himself something of an expert on the subject. The grin on Maynard's face was actually not that uncommon.

"Jimmy put you up to this, didn't he? He hired you for some commercial and thought it would be cute to send you up here and pretend to be a cop, right?"

Garrison reached into his jacket and pulled out his badge. Maynard grabbed it skeptically and looked at it.

"This is real," he whispered.

Garrison nodded.

"Donna's really dead?"

"Yes."

"Who…who did it?"

"We don't know just now. That's why I'm here."

"You don't think I did it, do you?"

"Not yet. Should we?"

"Of course not."

"Where were you yesterday?"

"At home. Doing some work."

"Can you prove it?"

Maynard thought about this for a moment. "No, I can't," he admitted. A panicked look took over his face. "Does that mean that—"

"Don't worry. At this point we have no reason to suspect you, and if we arrested and convicted somebody every time they couldn't prove where they were when something happened, our jobs would be a lot easier. The reason I'm here is just so I can get a picture of the victim and an idea of who might've wanted to harm her. I already know she didn't have any family to speak of, and her secretary said that you were the person closest to her."

Maynard seemed surprised by this. "That's so sad," he whispered.

"How do you mean?"

"It's just that we weren't that close. We only saw each other a couple of times a month, usually when one of us got lonely. We weren't really what you would call a couple. I don't even know that much about her."

"How did you guys meet?"

"About a year ago, I went to Lynden, Hunter and Associates to see Donald Mason, my divorce lawyer. Donna had started helping my lawyer with my divorce proceedings. She seemed fun, so I gave her my phone number and she called me a week later."

"You're divorced?"

"Yeah," Maynard nodded, "but it's funny. I was going there that day to tell Donald I wasn't going to need him anymore. Me and my ex-wife were planning to try to patch things up, but then I met Donna and decided I might as well play the field and get the divorce after all."

"Your ex couldn't have been too happy about that."

"No, she wasn't," Maynard admitted.

"Might she be the type of person to harbor a grudge?"

Maynard laughed out loud at this. "Jeanna? No. She's probably the least violent person on the planet. She wouldn't even let me kill spiders inside our house. I had to trap them and take them outside. That was one of the reasons I ended up divorcing her. It's exhausting being married to a saint."

"So even if she didn't do it herself, you don't think she might have hired someone to do it for her?"

Maynard's answer was unequivocal.

"No."

* * *

Garrison hated the morgue. He hated its smell and its constant chill. He also didn't like Hamilton, the balding, myopic lead examiner, whose years on the job had given him a jaunty indifference that Garrison found disrespectful and irritating.

They stood beside the table that held Donna's body, and Hamilton went over what he had found.

"I can't say I've seen many like this before," he admitted. "The bruising on her body was obviously caused by a fairly large man, but the wounds that killed her seem to have been caused by a large animal."

"I don't get you."

"At one point someone grabbed her, and he had a very tight grip. His fingers left bruises across her face, shoulders and neck. See?" Hamilton pointed to the dark marks that covered Donna's upper body. "Here, here and here."

"Any fingerprints?"

"A few. I already sent them in to be checked against the database."

Garrison nodded. It could take awhile for a match to be found, but finding fingerprints was good news.

"But what's this about an animal?" he asked.

"That's just it. She died because she bled to death from these three wounds." He pointed to three jagged-looking cuts. "These are the same kind of cuts you would find on someone who had been mauled by an animal. And to do this kind of damage it would have to be pretty big."

"How big?"

"We're talking lions, tigers and bears—oh my," Hamilton replied with a smirk.

In Homicide, all of a detective's cases were written on the whiteboard that dominated the division's left wall. Solved cases were written in black and unsolved cases were written in red. Garrison had the best record in the room. Only one red name sat under his. It had been a month since Donna Wendt was found murdered and he was no closer to solving the case than he had been that first day. Since then he had solved 12 other cases. Ten of them had been obvious—the killers had pretty much been caught with the knives in their hands—but the other two had taken him a couple of days and had distracted him from the Wendt case. Today, though, he had nothing else on his plate and he decided to pursue the one lead he had yet to check out.

Joshua Maynard had been positive that his ex-wife Jeanna could have had nothing to do with the murder, but as Garrison's list of possible suspects grew shorter and shorter, it became clear that he had to talk to her before making that decision for himself.

According to Maynard, she worked from home as an artist. Garrison found a website that showed some pictures of her work, and while it was clear that her paintings were never going to make her famous or sell for millions of dollars after her death, it wasn't hard to believe that she could make a good living producing them. Her style was impressionistic with hints of classicism. Three of the paintings he found were of the same subject, a large black German shepherd. The three paintings were all titled "Moses," and they were all loving portraits of the dog, who came across in them as friendly and happy. There was something slightly off about the dog's depiction, but Garrison couldn't figure out what it was.

It was close to lunchtime when he knocked on her door. From behind it he could hear the sound of a large dog barking. A few moments passed before the door opened.

Jeanna Maynard was a small, pretty woman, with short red hair that framed her face and little round glasses that brought attention to her startling green eyes. Garrison immediately understood why Joshua had found the idea of his ex-wife killing Donna so laughable. Standing in front of him she looked so petite and frail, he almost worried that the heavy oak door she held open might slip out of her grasp and shatter her as it slammed shut.

"Moses, be quiet!" she shouted at a barking dog Garrison couldn't see. "Can I help you?" she asked.

Garrison nodded. He grabbed his badge from his jacket pocket and showed it to her as he introduced himself.

"I'm here about what happened to a woman named Donna Wendt," he told her.

"Oh," she answered. "Then I guess you should come in."

Garrison walked in past her and she closed the door behind him. He turned into her living room and was immediately confronted by Moses, who growled threateningly at him.

"Moses, stop that!" ordered Jeanna, and the dog became quiet, but his eyes remained fixed on Garrison. "I'm sorry, he's not used to dealing with strangers."

Now that he could see the dog, Garrison realized why the paintings he had seen of the animal had seemed slightly off. Moses was missing his right ear and a long scar ran down from his forehead, between his eyes and down his muzzle.

"He looks pretty fierce," he remarked to Jeanna.

"Yeah, but once you get to know him, he's just the world's biggest sweetheart."

"That must have been some fight he was in."

"I don't know about that. He was just a puppy when it happened. That's how I got him, actually. Joshua and I had just come home from a dinner party when I heard this whimpering sound in the backyard. I went out to explore and I found this tiny little puppy lying beside our lawn furniture. He had been torn to pieces by some other animal. Joshua, humanitarian that he is, wanted to call somebody to come and take him away, but I insisted that we find a vet who could take care of him." She walked over to the big dog, which started to pant happily when she bent down and patted his fur. "He almost didn't make it, but we found somebody and he stitched him up and we took him home and took care of him. And he's been my loyal protector ever since." With a smile, she stood back up and offered to get Garrison a cup of coffee.

He shook his head. "No thanks. The caffeine keeps me up nights."

"Okay. Then what can I do for you?"

"I just have a few questions. I'm assuming you do know what happened to Ms. Wendt."

"Yes, I read about it in the paper. But that was awhile ago."

"Almost a month now."

"So I take it there were no obvious leads."

"No. That's why I'm here." Garrison paused as he tried to figure out the best way to start his questioning. It was unusual for him to hesitate, but there was something about Jeanna that made him cautious. He didn't want to upset her. She seemed like a good person. He cleared his throat before he spoke. "It's my understanding that you had cause to dislike Ms. Wendt."

"I didn't even know her. Not really."

"According to your ex-husband, she was responsible for him deciding to go on with the divorce."

"He was responsible for that. Donna was just a good excuse."

"So you didn't bear her any grudge?"

"By that time, our marriage was over. We talked about trying to start over, but we were just fooling ourselves. If it hadn't been Donna, it would have been somebody else." She paused for a second. "Am I to gather by this line of questioning that I'm a suspect?"

"I told you, we were out of leads."

"Okay," Jeanna nodded her head seriously, "then in the interest of full disclosure I should tell you that I did have a reason to hate her, but it had nothing to do with my divorce."

Garrison raised his eyebrows at this and she continued.

"When we got the divorce, we were obligated by law to split everything we owned evenly, including this house, which my great-grandfather built. The only way I could keep it was to agree to pay Joshua half its full market value, and I agreed. I obviously couldn't pay him in one lump sum, so we agreed on a set monthly payment. Unfortunately, this isn't the best time to be in the art market and over the past few months I've been having trouble making my payments. What I didn't know when I signed the agreement was that Donna had inserted a clause into it that said that if I repeatedly defaulted on my payments, then full ownership of the house would go to Joshua and he could do with it what he liked. Now Joshua can be a jerk, but I know he wouldn't actually do that to me. But I do know that Donna was trying to convince him that he was in the right to take my house away, so I was kind of peeved at her about that."

"But you didn't kill her."

"Of course not."

Hours later as Garrison went over his notes he tried to figure out what had happened during his discussion with Jeanna. She was his last and best suspect and she had supplied him with an excellent motive for her to want to see Donna Wendt dead. Like her ex-husband, she claimed to have been at home when the murder occurred but had no way to prove it. The medical examiner had told him that Wendt had died from wounds caused by a large animal, and there was Moses, as big a dog as Garrison had ever seen. All the pieces fit, but he remained unconvinced. Like most detectives he had developed a sixth sense about these things, and his was telling him that Jeanna was innocent, despite all the evidence to the contrary.

The best piece of physical evidence they had, the fingerprints found on Wendt's body, had gone unmatched in the database. Whoever the prints belonged to had never been charged with anything before. Jeanna hadn't gotten so much as a traffic ticket in her entire life. He couldn't imagine her being strong enough to hold someone down and leave those bruises, but he had seen stranger things in his day. Hate was a powerful thing and it could make weak people strong and strong people weak. As he went to sleep that night, he tossed and turned as he debated the possibility that his instincts were wrong and Jeanna really did kill her ex-husband's sometime girlfriend.

The call that woke him up the next morning erased all doubt from his mind. As he got dressed, he cursed himself for having been fooled by the charisma of a fragile beauty. Inside an expensive apartment 20 blocks away was proof that Jeanna had to be the one.

Jenson was already there when Garrison walked in. The body of Joshua Maynard lay beside a white leather couch on a once-white carpet. Jenson turned to the detective when he noticed that he was there.

"Ever try to get blood out of a white carpet?" he asked with a dark smile, which Garrison did not return.

"What happened here?" he asked with a stony expression on his face.

"Nothing unusual. The victim was preparing to go to bed when someone broke in. They struggled, and he" —he cocked his head towards Maynard— "lost."

Garrison bent over and took a look at Maynard's corpse. The wounds that covered his back and chest were identical to those that had been found on Donna Wendt.

Two uniformed officers backed up Garrison as he knocked on the door to Jeanna's house. Moses began to bark from inside and after a moment Jeanna opened the door.

"Detective Garrison," she said, seeming surprised to see him. "What can I do for you?"

"I'm afraid I have to ask you to come with us and answer some questions," he said without any emotion.

"Why? What's wrong? Has something happened?"

"Your ex-husband has been murdered."

Jeanna stared at him with a look of utter disbelief. "Joshua's dead?" she managed as tears began to form in her eyes.

"Yes, he is."

Moses' barks continued, growing louder and more violent.

"And you think I did it."

"I just need you to come in and answer some questions."

"Am I under arrest?"

"No, but you will be if you refuse to come with us."

Jeanna looked at him and nodded quietly.

"Moses, be quiet!" she shouted at her dog while she grabbed her coat and left with Garrison and the officers.

Garrison had to let Jeanna go. Although he was convinced that she was responsible, her fingerprints didn't match those found at the two crime scenes and a lack of any other evidence made it impossible for an arrest to be made. Although this meant she had not been there when the murders happened, it didn't mean she hadn't orchestrated the crimes.

As soon as he let her go, he began to follow her every move and studied her phone records. The weeks passed and it became clear that Jeanna was a lonely woman. Apart from her art dealer and telemarketers, she spoke to no one on the phone. She had no Internet access and she seldom left her house except to take Moses for his daily walk and to run errands. Garrison grew frustrated as his surveillance turned up no new evidence and no sign of a conspirator.

Two months after her murder, Donna Wendt's name was still written in red on the whiteboard, as was Joshua Maynard's, but as Garrison left the precinct that night he felt confident that Jeanna would slip up at some point and that he would catch her. It was a warm, quiet night. Garrison looked up and saw a bright full moon in the night sky. He walked over to his car and was about to open its door when he heard someone approach him from behind. He turned slowly and in the darkness he saw a tall, muscular man with skin as dark as ebony. The man was naked and a long scar ran down his face. He had only one ear.

Before Garrison could say or do anything, the stranger in front of him grabbed him and threw him to the ground. He spoke in a voice that barely seemed human. It was more a growl translated into very basic English.

"Should have left her alone!" yelled the stranger, giving Garrison a glimpse of his sharp white teeth. Garrison looked down at the hands that kept him from getting up and fighting back. At the ends of the fingers were nails so thick and sharp they could only be called claws.

He looked into the man's eyes and knew that he had seen them before.

"Moses?" he asked, not believing what he was seeing.

The man said nothing. Instead he held Garrison down with one arm while he raised the other. For a second, moonlight shone on his claws before he brought them down to the detective's throat.

Garrison tried to scream, but all he could manage was a garbled moan. The man's claws sliced into him over and over again until he was silent.

Satisfied, the man stood up and looked down at what he had done. A happy smile took over his face, and he began to run away from the lifeless body of the detective. He felt such joy as he ran it was all he could do not to shout out with glee. He ran for a long time before he finally made it back home. He walked into his backyard and stood outside her bedroom window and watched her as she slept. She looked so peaceful. Over the past few months she had been having trouble sleeping, because of her fears about her losing her house and the trouble she had had from the police, but that was all over now and she was going to be okay.

He stood there for hours, until finally the sun began to rise. He was used to the pain by now and kept himself from screaming as his bones shrank and his muscles contracted. His body contorted and hair began to sprout all over him. His face changed and was no longer human. Within a minute he was back to his regular self.

Wanting to be fed, he walked over to the back door and scratched it with his paw until Jeanna got up and let him in.

"How'd you get out?" she asked him as he walked in past her. He went into the kitchen and sat by his bowls. She followed him in and filled them up with food and water. He was very hungry and thirsty, so he ate and drank quickly. She made herself a cup of coffee and sat at the kitchen table and began to read from her newspaper. When he finished eating he walked over to her and put his head in her lap. She put down her paper and smiled and began to rub and stroke him around his head and neck.

"Who's a good boy?" she asked him. "Who's a good boy?"

He didn't answer her; he just stayed quiet and panted happily.

Jeremy's Summer

This summer wasn't like the others Jeremy had spent at his grandmother's. It didn't speed away in a blaze of time that went by so fast the days bled into each other and weeks ended before you realized they had even begun. Instead it passed slowly and wistfully and left the young boy with plenty of time to finish all the projects he had dreamed about during the long school year. Jeremy assumed that this slow passage of time was because this year it was just he and his grandmother staying at her beautiful seaside home. His parents had decided to go somewhere else for their vacation, and this couldn't have pleased him more. He loved his parents, but they always had plans about what to do during the day and he preferred to just wake up and find things to do on his own. Of all the summers he could remember, this one was easily the best.

Jeremy was 10 and was completely normal for his age. He was the right size and the right weight and he had ordinary brown eyes and short brown hair. His imagination was both as simple and as complicated as that of his peers, overtaken as it was by tales of supermen and dinosaurs and robots a hundred feet tall. The only thing that was extraordinary about him was how completely average he was.

His grandmother, on the other hand, was an extraordinary person. She was 68 but could easily pass as someone 20 years younger, thanks to her high cheekbones and the slim figure she kept as a result of her many different hobbies. Her hair was a brilliant silver, and she always kept it looking modern, not wanting to be one of those women who wore the same hairstyle as when they were 40. She was fun and energetic, but she always knew when to leave Jeremy alone and let him play by himself. She was an excellent baker and Jeremy had come to look forward to the Fridays when she would bake cookies. She never made the same kind twice and she never yelled at him when he stole one from the counter while they cooled. With one exception, she never lost her temper. She would scold him when he misbehaved, but she never became frightening or impatient, except on those rare occasions when he tried to go into the basement.

It had been a super lazy day and Jeremy had become bored playing with his miniature cars in his bedroom. With a tired sigh he had lifted himself off the floor and walked downstairs with the hopes of persuading his grandmother to play a couple of rounds of "go fish" with him, but as he walked around the house it became clear she wasn't there. He looked outside, because she had recently taken up watercolors and liked to paint the view from her backyard, but she wasn't there either. He started shouting for her, but she didn't respond to his calls. The only place where he thought she could be was the basement, a place she had warned him about many times. She had told him that it was as dark as night down there and that there were things inside it that dreamed of eating little boys. While this may have fooled him when he was seven or eight, Jeremy was now old enough to know that she was probably just trying to scare him with her tales of monsters and the dark. Still, as mature as he was, he had to admit that she had done a very good job. Jeremy hated the dark, and his fear of what could hide in its claustrophobic blackness had kept him, despite his growing curiosity, from exploring the one part of the house that had been declared off limits.

But there was something about being alone in the house on this quiet day that allowed his courage to build and, after he had checked out every other available nook and cranny and still failed to find his grandmother, he decided that today was the day to discover the truth. Although he was apparently alone in the house, he still crept guiltily towards the door, as if at any time his granny could jump out of nowhere and catch him in the act. He made it to the door and grabbed its doorknob, but before he could turn it, it began to turn all by itself. He let go and stepped away from the door, which opened slowly and revealed a tall slim figure.

"What are you doing?!" his grandmother shouted at him as she appeared from the darkness that surrounded the basement's entrance, causing his heart to almost stop and his body to physically jump in the air with fright.

"I—" He tried to explain that he was just looking for her, but she didn't want to hear his excuses.

"What did I tell you about the basement?" she yelled as she turned and locked the basement's door with a key Jeremy had never seen before.

He looked down at the floor and shuffled his bare feet with a mixture of shame and embarrassment. "I'm not supposed to go in there," he mumbled to his toes.

"That's right!"

He had never heard her sound so angry before. He couldn't understand why she was so mad.

"Now go to your room and stay there until you can learn to understand the rules!"

With his head hung in shame, Jeremy trudged back upstairs to his room and went back to joylessly playing with his toy cars while he pondered his grandmother's strange change in demeanor. He was too young to understand that what he interpreted as her wrath was instead a very palpable fear. There was something in that basement that scared her, and she did not want Jeremy to find out what it was.

A couple of hours later she knocked on his door to tell him that she had just made some triple chocolate chip peanut-butter cookies and that he could come out and have one if he wanted. To Jeremy's surprise, he said no thanks. For the first time in his life he didn't want a cookie.

Clearly guilt-stricken by her outburst, she returned to his door several times with offers of a game of cards, a video and a trip in her canoe. He said no thanks to all of them and stayed in his room, imagining what would have to be in the basement to make it off limits. First he thought of the monsters he had seen on television, the vampires and the werewolves and the zombies stitched together out of other people's spare parts. Then he thought of the dangers his parents always warned him about, like the strangers who carried candy and the neighbor's dog that didn't play well with children. He imagined that the basement was filled with a thousand different natural dangers, like quicksand, lava and poisonous snakes. The more he thought about the basement, the more excited he became. In his mind he envisioned every adventure that was denied to a 10-year-old, and even though he knew there was no way any of these things could be down there, he was overcome by curiosity about what really was.

Eventually his granny was able to coax him out of his room with an offer of hot dogs for supper. As he slathered his wiener with mustard and relish, his thoughts of the basement vanished and stayed away for the rest of the day.

The next morning, though, proved to be just as lazy and humdrum as the one before it, and Jeremy battled boredom by dreaming up a way to get into the basement. He spent the whole morning lying on his bedroom floor and imagining new things he might find down there, before he became distracted by one of his action figures and decided to engage his plastic troops in a massive battle.

This became the pattern he followed through the next week and a half. Jeremy would get up and start thinking about the basement and how he could get in there, but before he could make good on his plans he would find something else to do and the day would pass with his curiosity still unsatisfied. He now watched his grandmother much more carefully than he had before. Having dreamed of a thousand different reasons he couldn't go down there, he now began to wonder what kind of person would keep those things in her home. He started following her and watched for any suspicious behavior, like her returning from the store with a large plastic bag of strange meat or a jumbo-sized doggy bone to feed what was down there, but nothing she did seemed very out of the ordinary. The only thing he noticed was that around 11 in the morning every Tuesday, she would slip into the basement. Twenty minutes later she would come back out, always with a look of wistful regret. Jeremy could tell that whatever she did down there, it made her sad.

Finally, after seemingly endless days of daydreaming and planning, Jeremy decided that he could wait no longer. He simply had to find out what was down there. To do that he would have to find out where his grandmother kept the key that opened the basement door. He spent the next two days searching around the house, with no success. While she was out painting in the backyard, he sneaked into her bedroom and went through her drawers. In one of them he came across a framed picture of himself with his grandmother and his parents. He remembered that it had been taken just before his parents left for their vacation. He wondered why she kept the picture in a drawer and not on a table somewhere, where everyone could see it. As he looked at it, it occurred to him that his parents hadn't called him once over the course of the summer. Tears came to his eyes when he suddenly realized how much he missed them. His grandmother had told him that there were no phones where they'd gone, and they had kept in touch by sending him postcards, but he still longed to hear their voices and feel the warmth of their bodies as they enveloped him in a good long hug. Hoping she wouldn't notice, he took the picture out of its frame and slipped it into his pocket. He put the frame back and searched the rest of the drawers for the key, but he came up empty.

With a knot of impatience and desire tightening in his stomach, Jeremy realized that the only way to find out where she kept the key would be to see her getting it. He had to wait three very long and boring days before the next Tuesday arrived. When it did, he sprang out of bed and dressed in what he believed was his most inconspicuous outfit, a black T-shirt and a pair of camouflage pants. While there was no foliage to hide in inside the house, he was still convinced his clothes would help keep him out of sight. Before he left his room, he retrieved the picture he had taken from his grandmother's room and looked at it before he folded it carefully and put it into his pocket. He had spent a lot of time over the past few days looking at that picture and there was something about it that didn't seem right. He didn't know what it was, but there was something about the way his grandmother looked that didn't seem normal.

His heart racing with excitement, he left his room and joined his grandmother downstairs, where she already had his breakfast of bacon and pancakes on his special plate. With a look of deliberate nonchalance he poured a mountain of syrup over everything and ate slowly, his eyes never once leaving his grandmother's figure.

"Is something wrong, Jeremy?" she asked him, having noticed the way he was watching her.

"Nope," Jeremy answered as he tried to figure out how the woman in front of him was different from the woman in the photograph.

"Are you sure?"

"Uh-huh."

They both finished eating and she gathered their plates, washed them and cleaned up the kitchen while Jeremy sat and watched her.

"You can go watch a video if you want," she told him. Usually he ran off as soon as she picked up his plate, but today he just shook his head and watched her.

"Do you want to help me?" she asked.

He nodded, then got up and grabbed a dry dishtowel and rubbed it against the wet plates she had just washed off. He was unusually quiet, and his eyes never left her.

When they finished cleaning up, she went to gather her easel and paints and set them up outside. He followed her, and she assumed that he was just feeling lonely, so she chatted with him as she began to paint, but he stayed quiet and responded with only one- or two-word answers.

"You're acting strange today," she told him.

He just shrugged, and she stopped talking to him.

An hour and a half passed before she quit painting and put everything away. It was almost 11 AM.

"Jeremy," she said to him, "I've got an errand I have to do, so could you do me a favor and go to your room and play with your toys in there for a while?"

He nodded silently and went into the house.

She went back into the house and slipped the supplies into a hallway cupboard. Before she closed it, she looked around to make sure that the coast was clear. Satisfied that she was alone, she pulled out what looked like a bottle of aerosol air freshener. She unscrewed its top and turned it upside down. A key fell out of its empty interior and into her hand. She screwed the top back onto the can and put it back into the cupboard. She then closed the cupboard and walked to the basement door, opened it and disappeared down its steps.

Jeremy couldn't believe he had gone so long without making a noise. He had spent the whole time crouching behind a chair in the living room. It faced the hallway, and he saw where his grandmother hid the key. As quietly as he could, he walked to his room and waited for night to fall, both excited and terrified that he would at last find out the truth.

When she came back from the basement 20 minutes later, Jeremy's grandmother noticed that the boy's strange demeanor had vanished and that he seemed to be back to his normal playful self. She allowed herself to stop worrying and spent the rest of the day pursuing her different hobbies.

After dinner they watched a video about the adventures of a group of animated dinosaurs and then it was time for bed. Jeremy's grandmother tucked him in and kissed him on his forehead, as she always did, and he smiled and wished her good night. She then turned out his lights and closed his door on her way out. As soon as she was gone, he reached over to his little bedside table and pulled out a small flashlight from its cupboard. He turned it on underneath his covers and used it to once again study the picture of his family. As he stared at it, he finally figured out why his grandmother looked so strange in it. She looked younger, and not just a little bit. This wasn't the result of fortunate lighting or well-applied makeup, but a genuine difference in age. The picture had been taken at the beginning of that summer, but the woman in the picture had to be at least 10 years younger. Her face was less wrinkled and her hair still had patches that had not yet turned gray.

This discovery led Jeremy to only one possible conclusion: the woman who had just tucked him in was not his grandmother. Sometime during the summer, she had replaced his real grandmother. He remembered the video he had once watched at his friend Alex's house. They had gotten only halfway through it before Alex's mom turned it off, saying it wasn't appropriate for kids their age. It was about how a group of aliens had started to take over people's bodies and assume their identities. It was now clear to him that an alien had snatched his grandmother's body and that its natural alien life span caused it to age faster than a normal human. Downstairs in the basement there was either some kind of spaceship or, he hoped, his still-alive real grandmother.

He waited for several torturous hours before he crept out of bed and slowly opened his door, which still managed to creak despite his best efforts. As quietly as he could, he tiptoed along the upstairs hallway and down the stairs. Each little noise he made sounded like a horrible cannon blast to his ears, and after each one he would freeze and make sure that he hadn't woken the alien up. He got downstairs and slowly made his way to the hallway cupboard. He opened it and, using his flashlight, found the fake aerosol can in which the key was hidden. Unfortunately, it was on the top shelf and he couldn't reach it. Having gone too far to stop, he went to the kitchen and grabbed one of the light plastic chairs that sat around the table. He lifted it up and carried it to the cupboard without making a sound. He stood on it and grabbed the aerosol can. It was hard to unscrew the top, but he finally managed to do it and retrieved the key. He slowly got off the chair and walked towards the basement door.

Though his movements were slow and deliberate, Jeremy's heart was beating so fast he could feel it thumping in his chest. He tried to calm himself down as he slipped the key into the doorknob, but the thought of what he was going to find behind the door was so thrilling and scary, his heart began to race even faster. He turned the key and opened the door. All he saw before him was darkness. He shone his small flashlight into it, but the darkness was so vast it quickly swallowed up all the light. Jeremy tried to find a light switch at the top of the stairs, but there was none.

Jeremy was suddenly overcome with the desire to close the door and run back to his room, but he fought this urge and slowly stepped into the darkness. He made his way down the stairs, which felt old and splintery against his stockinged feet. He moved his flashlight around and caught only glimpses of a dirt floor and stone walls. It was cold and he felt goose bumps rise out of his skin. He listened for any signs of life, but heard only the house's normal quiet moans and creaks. He got to the last step and felt the coldness of the floor as he stepped onto it. He turned and with his flashlight caught a glimpse of a string hanging in front of him. He reached out for it, found it and gave it a sharp tug. All at once the basement filled with light, and Jeremy saw that there was no spaceship and no sign of his real grandmother. Instead all he saw was a large ornate rectangular box surrounded by about a dozen unlit candles.

Jeremy had seen coffins before, but this one seemed way too small. Unless it was built for a midget he couldn't think of any adult who could fit inside it. He had started to walk towards it when he heard his grandmother's voice.

"Jeremy, don't," she said softly, her voice full of sadness and regret.

Jeremy whirled and saw her standing at the foot of the basement stairs. She was dressed in her nightgown and she didn't look angry at all. There were tears in her eyes and it looked as if she was shaking.

"Granny, what is that?" he asked her, confused and frightened by her sadness.

An avalanche of grief overcame her face and she began to sob. Her legs weakened and she sat down on the basement steps. Jeremy forgot all about his alien theory and rushed over to comfort her. He wrapped his arms around her and she hugged him as tightly as she could.

"It's okay," he whispered to her, "you don't have to tell me."

Hearing this, she managed to stop crying and shook her head.

"No. It's time that you found out. It's too soon for me, but it is still time."

With the sleeve of her nightgown, she wiped away her tears and motioned for Jeremy to sit beside her on the step. They sat like that together for several minutes before she found the strength to speak.

"You were so young," she finally managed. "I wasn't ready to let you go. John and Shari had led a good life. They had found each other and had you, so even though I missed them so much, I could accept that they were gone, but you were just a child. You had been robbed of a life, and I had been robbed of all the time we could have had together."

"I don't understand," Jeremy whispered to her.

"The three of you had come over here for just two days. Usually you would come here for the whole summer, but that year you three were going to go to Hawaii. You spent the night and left the next morning for the airport. On the way there, you were hit by a semi driven by a trucker who had been on the road for 40 hours straight. No one survived."

Jeremy just stared at her. She wasn't making any sense to him.

"For six months after that I was consumed with grief. You had been stolen from me and I would do anything to get you back. And anything is what I did."

She paused for a long moment before she continued.

"I started studying books about magic and the paranormal. I became obsessed with the idea that I could bring you back, but the more I studied the more it became clear that a complete resurrection would be impossible, so I settled for the next best thing. I went to the graveyard where you were buried and I dug out your coffin. I brought it back here and each week, on the day and at the hour that the accident occurred, I perform a ceremony that summons your spirit and brings you to this house."

Jeremy shook his head. He began to speak, but she gently grabbed his head and whispered to him.

"Jeremy," she tried her best to sound brave and comforting, "you're a ghost."

He began to cry. "No," he insisted, "that's not true. You're lying."

"No." She kissed his forehead. "I'm not."

"I want my mom and dad," he began to sob.

"I know you do," she said, hugging him to her side, "but they're gone."

"The postcards," he protested.

"I sent those."

"That's not true. You're lying to me. Aliens lie."

"Aliens?"

"You're an alien!" He grabbed the photograph from out of one of his pajama pockets. "See, you don't look like my grandmother."

His grandmother took the photograph from his hand and smiled sadly.

"We took this the morning before you left that day. I do look different, don't I?"

"Yeah," Jeremy sniffled.

"This picture was taken 10 years ago."

"No, it wasn't. We took it at the start of this summer."

Jeremy's grandmother nodded sadly, and suddenly Jeremy knew that she was right and everything she said was true.

"I'm sorry," he apologized.

"For what?"

"I shouldn't have gone into the basement."

"That's okay."

They sat quietly on the step for several minutes before she spoke again. "It's time that I let you go."

"What?" He didn't understand.

"I've kept you here long enough. It's time that I let you pass on."

"You don't want me here?"

"Of course I want you here, but now that you know the truth don't you want to leave?"

"Why would I want to do that?"

"Well, you could see your parents for a start."

Jeremy thought about this. "But can't I wait until the summer ends?"

"Of course you can, if that's what you want," his grandmother smiled.

"That's what I want."

His grandmother began to cry once again, but this time her tears were full of joy. When she finished crying, the two of them stood up and went to their rooms and went back to bed. The next morning they got up and did not say a word to each other about what had happened the previous night. The decades passed and the summer continued and as it did Jeremy's grandmother began to look nothing like the woman in the picture. She became weaker, her skin became more wrinkled and she grew thinner. Eventually she spent most of her days in bed, where Jeremy kept her company by playing "go fish" and listening to her stories. She always got up on Tuesday mornings, though, until finally she could not get up at all.

Jeremy cried when he found her. He called 911 and hid away when they came. They took her away, and Jeremy spent a lonely week inside the empty house. The summer was ending and slowly, as the days passed, he began to fade away. On the last day, he lay down on his bed and closed his eyes to sleep. When he opened them, he saw his grandmother standing above him. She looked much younger than he had ever seen her before, but it was definitely she. Behind her he saw his parents. They looked just like he remembered them. Jeremy smiled. As he sat up he knew that this dream would last even longer than the summer had.

Fetaboy

Not only was it a very busy night when Mark snapped, but it had also been the hottest day of the year. The kitchen at Yiorgos' Taverna could get uncomfortably hot during even the coldest winter, so when it was 105 degrees in the shade the small open space was as close to hell as any living person could stand. Sweat poured down his face and blurred his vision. Order after order kept coming in. No matter how hard the four cooks worked to get the food out, they were always behind and the waiters yelled at them because the customers were getting impatient.

Mark had come to hate the customers, especially the ones who couldn't seem to comprehend that they were not the only ones in the restaurant. He hated the way they sent food back, even though he made sure not to include any green peppers as they had asked. He hated the way they yelled and screamed and laughed when the belly dancer came out. Gina, the perpetually chipper redhead who worked beside him, would always catch him scowling and nudge him with a wink.

"Relax, buddy," she'd grin, "they're just having fun."

Whenever she said this to him, he would just frown and concentrate on getting the appetizers out. What Gina didn't understand was that the reason he hated them was they were having fun. He resented that their joy came at the expense of his hard work and that the only time they acknowledged him was to tell him that their calamari was too soggy.

Still, as much as he had grown to hate the customers, they weren't what made him snap that night. Nor did it have anything to do with the heat or the constant stress. He snapped because of something the new girl said to him.

Her name was Emma, and like all the waitresses hired by Jenny, the owner's wife, she was a pretty young girl, just out of high school and on her way to university. She had long blonde hair and a knowing confidence. Over the past three weeks that she had worked at the taverna, she had had little occasion to speak to Mark other than to give him dinner orders.

What she didn't know—what no one at the taverna knew—was that Mark wasn't a well person, mentally speaking. He was a diagnosed schizophrenic with the emotional tendencies of a sociopath. He had spent the last 10 years of his life in and out of hospitals but had taken a turn for the better when his doctors found the right medication to treat his illness. He hadn't told George, the restaurant's owner, about his illness when he was hired, but he was at his healthiest back then and his behavior was perfectly normal. It wasn't until around the time that Emma was hired that he started to slip. The reason for this was simple: he had stopped taking his medication. He had come to believe that he had been completely cured and that he no longer needed to take the drugs that had made him well.

Before he worked at the restaurant, back when he was still in the hospital, he believed that he was the chosen savior of the world, a man-shaped deity known as the Phaetaboi. As the Phaetaboi it was his responsibility to protect the world from the clutches of an insidious global cabal known as the League of the Serpent. These evil men and women were dedicated to the destruction of Western civilization and were intent on destroying it from within. Mark had been convinced that virtually anybody could be a member of the league, and that he, as their greatest nemesis, was always at risk of being exposed and assassinated. When he left the hospital he managed to leave this fantasy behind him, but now, as the effects of his medication began to wear off, the delusion began to take hold of his mind once again.

It started when he began to wonder if any of his coworkers were members of the league. While he could never be sure, he had dismissed the majority of them as being too decent to be secretly evil. There was something about the new girl, however, that made her a suspect. She was a blonde and most of them were blondes. She was pretty and most of them were somehow attractive (all the better to lure innocents into their thrall), and her tongue was sharp, just like a serpent's.

Because of his suspicions, he started to keep an eye on Emma, watching her whenever he didn't think she was looking. His surveillance, though, did not go unobserved. Emma started to wonder why the tall, creepy appetizer guy was always looking at her. It was when she finally called him on it that he snapped.

It was near the end of the night and the restaurant was slowly emptying out. The wait staff started cleaning up and the kitchen was closing down. Before they could start cleaning up, the cooks had to prepare for the next day, which was going to be just as busy. Mark noticed that they were low on crumbled feta and so, as he had hundreds of times before, he took out some blocks of cheese and started to squish them down with the thick end of a butcher knife. Emma was right in front of him, cleaning off a table, so he started to stare at her, looking for some sign of her allegiance to evil. She noticed him immediately and decided she'd had enough. With her hands on her hips she turned towards him and looked directly into his eyes.

"What are *you* looking at, Fetaboy?"

Mark's blood froze and his heart stopped. She had just called him by his true name, Phaetaboi. Only a member of the League of the Serpent would know who he really was. He had been right all along. Emma was evil and had obviously been sent to the restaurant on a mission to kill him. He would not let that happen.

With a scream of rage and fury he ran from behind the counter of the open kitchen with the large butcher knife still in his hand. Emma could see the anger that burned in his eerie green eyes and instantly knew that he meant to kill her. She screamed and began to run to the other end of the restaurant, hoping to escape out the front door. Mark chased after her, but he was stopped when Dan, a quick-thinking waiter, threw a chair in front of him. Mark tripped over the chair and fell hard on the floor, where he landed on the butcher knife. For a moment it seemed as if he was okay, but then blood began to seep out from underneath him. Dan and George rushed to him and turned him over, while Jenny called for an ambulance. Her effort was wasted, though, because the knife had severed a major artery and Mark was dead by the time the paramedics made it to the restaurant.

The police arrived, and for a moment George worried that they would force him to close down the restaurant for several days while they investigated the accident. The truth was that this week was so important to his business that a couple of days could literally mean having to shut it down permanently. He was visibly relieved when the officers came to him a few hours later and told him that there was no reason for him not to open tomorrow. He briefly worried that the news of the accident might keep people away, but he forgot about that when he realized that he needed a fourth cook for the following night.

When Al walked into the restaurant the next morning, he had no idea what had happened the night before. The previous day had been his day off, and he had spent it sleeping and watching reruns on television. So the last thing he expected to see was Jenny and George mopping up what looked like dry blood from the floor.

Stunned, Al took off his sunglasses and walked over to them. "What happened?" he asked them.

"Mark had an accident," George answered.

"Is he okay?"

Jenny and George looked down and continued mopping.

"No," George answered, "no, he's not."

"Is he in the hospital?"

"No."

That was how Al found out he had been promoted from dishwasher to cook.

Al had never worn chef's whites before, and he found the uniform hot and uncomfortable compared to the plain white shirt he wore in the dish pit. He had spent enough time in the kitchen that he knew where everything was, and he received a crash course in how to prepare all the different salads and appetizers, but that still did little to calm his nerves. He had never cooked before and he was going to have to learn on one of the busiest days of the year. He felt as if someone had handed him a parachute while mumbling something about the rip cord and then pushed him out of an airplane. Gina understood his anxiety and took him under her wing.

"You'll be fine," she smiled. "You're the best dishwasher we've got and that's just as hard as this is."

Al nodded and tried to stay calm as people started to arrive and be seated.

"Al," he heard someone say his name. It was George.

"Yeah?"

"I think we're going to need some more feta." George pointed to the metal insert in front of Al. It was only half full. For some reason the feta Mark had crumbled the night before had been thrown away.

"Okay," Al answered. He walked over to where the cheese was kept and found that the space was empty. That meant he had to go downstairs to get some.

The restaurant's basement was where the large walk-in freezer and refrigerator were kept. It was a dark place, mostly because no one could be bothered to replace its burned-out fluorescent light bulbs. It also contained a large wrought-iron cage where extra chairs, dishes and cutlery were kept, a locked room that contained all the restaurant's booze and two changing rooms for the employees. The machine that operated the cold storage units rattled and hummed constantly with a noise that reminded Al of insects in a tropical jungle. He had spent so much time down there over the six months he had worked at Yiorgos' that he no longer noticed its creepy atmosphere.

He opened the refrigerator door, walked in and looked for the large white pail that contained the white blocks of feta cheese. He found it, opened it and grabbed two large blocks to take upstairs. As he stood up, the refrigerator door slammed shut in front of him.

"What the—" Al started, caught unawares by the sudden action. "Is somebody out there?" he asked aloud.

No one answered him.

Al rolled his eyes and assumed that this was some sort of prank. The other cooks liked to haze the newcomers on their first day, but Al had worked with them for half a year so he had thought he'd be exempt from this foolishness.

With the cheese in his hands he walked over to the door and tried to push it open with his foot. The door was designed so it was impossible for anyone to become locked inside the unit, but the door would not budge as he pushed against it. With a sigh he put the cheese down on the metal shelf to his right and pushed against the door with his entire body. It still would not open.

"This isn't funny, guys!" he shouted through the door. "We're way too busy for this."

Even though he could feel someone pushing the door closed on the other side, he couldn't hear any sounds. Normally they would all be unsuccessfully stifling giggles while doing something like this. He pushed as hard as he could, but whoever was on the other side pushed harder and kept the door closed. Al started to get angry.

"Open the door!" he shouted.

There was no response.

"Fine," he yelled, swearing as he walked to the back of the refrigerator. He put his back to its cold wall and started to jump up and down to get his blood flowing. He breathed in deeply and then ran screaming towards the door. Just as he was about to hit it, it opened up and he ran straight into the wall beyond with a loud and painful crash. He fell to the floor and tried to catch his breath while he lay flat on his back.

"What are you doing?" George stared down at him incredulously.

Al found this question annoying and turned it around on his boss.

"What are *you* doing? Do you usually play pranks on your cooks?"

"Pranks? What pranks?"

Al got up and walked into the refrigerator and grabbed the cheese he needed. "Holding the door closed so I couldn't get out," he answered.

"What are you talking about? I just came down here to see what was keeping you so long. People are starting to order."

Al walked out of the unit and closed its door. "You mean it wasn't you keeping me in there?"

"Are you kidding? I don't have time for that crap."

"Then who was it?"

George looked at him as if he were brain damaged. With a look of exasperation he spoke as calmly and patiently as he could. "It was no one. Now go upstairs and get that cheese crumbled."

Al had never been so hot in his life. It could get pretty sweaty in the dish pit, but that was nothing compared to this. Orders starting coming in so fast that his brain refused to process them. For a moment he just stopped moving and tried to catch his breath.

"What are you doing?" George shouted at him from the grill. "I need that salad, now!"

This got Al moving again and he put together a side salad. He found the roar that came from the customers distracting and he tried to ignore it, but it rang in his head and made it difficult to figure out what he had to do next. The strange incident in the refrigerator had occurred only an hour and a half ago, but already it seemed like ancient history—like something that happened to him in another life. His heart raced and sweat poured down from under his hat and stung his eyes.

Then—just like that—it stopped. Orders stopped coming in and Al and the rest of the cooks had a chance to relax a little. George disappeared into his office to watch the last period of a hockey game and left the other three cooks to handle the kitchen.

"You can take a break now if you want," Gina smiled at Al, who looked as though he was about to faint.

"Thanks," he mumbled as he took off his hat and walked to the back room where the staff went to get away from the customers. Once there he slumped down on a stool, crossed his arms and put his head down on the room's large white counter. He was like this when Dan, the waiter, came in to grab a cigarette.

"You look rough," he noted sympathetically.

Al just groaned. He turned his head and looked at Dan, who seemed uncharacteristically nervous and fidgety.

"Are you okay?" he asked.

Dan shrugged. "I shouldn't have come in to work today," he admitted. "I'm still a little freaked out by what happened with Mark. Emma was smart enough to take the day off."

"What did happen?" asked Al.

"Didn't they tell you?"

"They told me he accidentally fell on a knife, but they didn't say how or why."

Dan nodded and then, as he smoked his cigarette, he told Al the whole story about what had happened that night.

"Fetaboy?" Al asked incredulously. "Why would something like that set him off?"

"Who knows? Mark was just a weird guy, I guess."

Dan stubbed out his cigarette in an ashtray and Al got up to get back to work. It then occurred to him that this was the first time since he'd arrived at the restaurant for his shift that someone had talked about what had happened that previous night. He wondered how it was possible for his coworkers to have witnessed something like that and not talk about it. When he got back to the kitchen, Gina pointed to the metal insert that he had filled with feta only two hours ago.

"You're almost out," she showed him. "You better get some more."

It was then that Al realized that crumbling stinky salty cheese was probably going to be his main duty at the restaurant from now on. He sighed and remembered that there still weren't feta blocks upstairs, which meant another trip to the basement.

Only now was he able to think about what had happened earlier in the day. When he got to the basement, he grabbed a heavy box from the cage, carried it to the walk-in and used it to prop open the door. Then he walked over to the same pail as before and opened it up. One last block of cheese floated in the brine. As he lifted it out the phrase that had so enraged his predecessor rang in his head. It seemed disrespectful, but he couldn't help finding it a little funny.

"Fetaboy," he muttered, trying not to giggle as he looked at the block of cheese in his hand.

He threw the lid back onto the empty pail and had just lifted it up to take to Carlos the dishwasher when the light bulb above his head exploded with a loud pop. Before he could react, the lights from outside the refrigerator followed in suit. Shards of glass began to rain down from the ceiling and he was plunged into total darkness.

Before he could react, he heard the sound of footsteps on the broken glass. They were headed towards him.

"Hello?" he gulped nervously, aware that there was a presence in the basement that wasn't too keen to see him around.

The crunching grew louder and louder until Al could feel the heat of the person right next to him. Al took a step back, but the other person just moved closer.

"Do you need something?" Al asked blindly, hoping that this was all about a desire for some more green peppers or cucumbers.

"You have taken my place," a familiar male voice explained to him. "You have taken over my duties."

Al remained quiet. There was something in this man's voice that was ominous and frightened him. In his heart he knew to whom the voice belonged, but his more rational mind refused to believe it.

The man continued, "At first I didn't think you were worthy. I tried to keep you in here to stop you, but you have proved yourself and I am satisfied."

"W...w...what are talking about?" stuttered Al.

He felt a cold hand grab his shoulder. Even through his clothing he could feel how clammy it was. The man appeared to have leaned in, as his voice came from just inches away.

"You are now the Phaetaboi," the voice explained.

"I don't know what that means."

"It means," the voice whispered, "that you must kill her. She is one of them and she will destroy you if you don't."

"Al, are you down there?" Gina's voiced echoed from the stairs. "Could you also bring up a pail of onions?"

In that one second that Gina's voice distracted him, Al felt a horrible chill enter his body. He began to shake and cough, and he fell to the floor and cut himself on the broken glass. His body twitched and writhed as he fought to stop the pain that had exploded in his chest. It felt as though he had been stabbed with a long sharp knife, and it was so intense that rather than endure it, his mind shut down and left him unconscious on the floor.

A few minutes later Gina went down to check on him. She was shocked to find the basement completely dark, and she almost stumbled over his body as she walked into the refrigerator.

Al was still unconscious when the ambulance came to pick him up.

* * *

After this second incident, George had little choice but to shut the restaurant down for a few days. An electrician determined that the lights in the basement had exploded because of a sudden and powerful energy surge, but the doctors were having a more difficult time determining what had happened to Al. He woke up two days later and insisted that nothing was wrong with him. They ran a whole battery of tests and he turned out to be right. Except for a few stitches on the cuts from the broken glass, he looked and sounded completely normal and left the hospital a few hours later. Meanwhile, the electrician installed a tiny, but very expensive, device into the restaurant's electrical system and gave George a bill so big that he almost needed a stay in the hospital himself.

Three days later, on a Thursday, the restaurant opened its doors once again, although there was some question whether anyone would want to eat there after all that had happened. Happily, it turned out that the restaurant's reputation for great food and good service was well enough established that people ignored the recent strange employee mishaps.

To the shock and surprise of the rest of the staff, Al came in that Thursday to work his shift in the kitchen. They all assumed he would want to take more time off. The other person they were surprised to see was Emma, who still seemed a bit shaken up by her encounter with the psychotic chef. The two of them happened to walk into the restaurant at the same time and were both greeted by an uneasy George.

"Hi guys," he managed to smile. "Try to take it easy today, okay?"

They both told him that they would do their best.

When Al went in to punch his time card, Gina walked over to him and asked him how he was doing.

"I'm fine," he mumbled to her antisocially as he walked past her towards the basement to change.

Even from that brief exchange, Gina could tell that something was different about Al. Not only in terms of attitude, but physically as well. Somehow he seemed slightly taller and darker. And his eyes, there was something wrong with his eyes, but she couldn't tell what.

Gina didn't know Al well enough to realize that his eyes were usually blue, but that now they were a strange and eerie green.

Inside the employee changing room, Emma wondered if she could actually work today. Her normally confident demeanor had been replaced by a tentative fragility since her encounter with Mark. She had never seen someone that angry before. He was ready to kill her, and the power of that hatred had given her horrible nightmares ever since the attack. In them Mark would appear to her as a seemingly solid but still strangely ethereal presence and speak to her in a low and threatening growl.

"You serpents may be strong," he hissed at her, "but the Phaetaboi is stronger. He cannot be slowed by something as trivial as death. Just when you think you are safe, he will appear in a guise you never once suspected. He will take you and your league of evil down to the hell where you were born!"

She had no idea what this was supposed to mean, but it frightened her and made her decision to come back to the restaurant a difficult one.

Knock. Knock.

The sound from the door made Emma jump.

"Just a sec," she called out.

"No hurry," a voice answered. It was Al.

Emma didn't really know Al that well. He was a quiet guy, and she had never sensed they had enough in common to get to know each other, so beyond the occasional "hello" and "good-bye" they almost never spoke to each other. But he seemed harmless, having little to nothing in common with Mark. She had never found him at all frightening or creepy.

She opened the changing room door and didn't even have a chance to scream before Al grabbed her and covered her mouth with a swath of duct tape. He pushed her back into the room and locked the door behind them. She fought against him, but although she was taller than he was, her blows did little good.

Al was sweating and when he spoke to her his voice sounded different. It was deeper and closer to the one that had been haunting her dreams. With a length of rope he tied her hands behind her back and threw her down roughly to the ground. Tears came to her eyes and she tried to scream when she saw him remove a large butcher knife from his backpack, but the tape muffled her cries.

"I told you," Al laughed at her menacingly. "I told you the Phaetaboi would have his revenge. You thought that by destroying my body you would win! But you forgot to destroy my spirit! I have returned, and for your crimes I will make you suffer!"

With that he raised the knife above his head, as Emma kicked and screamed and prayed for someone to save her. With a scream of primal fury he started to bring the knife down, but before it could slice into her flesh something stopped him. A force kept his hand from moving down any farther. He fought against it, but it was too strong and would not allow him to kill the helpless young woman.

"What is happening?" he cried out in anger.

From his own mouth the answer came, but this time the voice matched the body.

"I will not let you do this!" Al shouted at the spirit that had invaded his body. "I will not let you take control of me and kill Emma!"

Emma watched, amazed, as the forces in Al's body engaged each other in a battle of words.

"She is an evil one!" Mark's spirit insisted. "She is a disciple of the League of the Serpent and must be destroyed!"

"No, she's not," Al countered, "because there's no such thing!"

"Fool! They have blinded you with their charms."

"No, they haven't, because they don't exist!"

"Stop resisting me!"

"No!"

Emma watched as the two spirits in the one body in front of her dropped the large knife. They then took control of different sides of the body and moved their fight into the realm of the physical. From the best that she could tell, Mark controlled the left side and Al controlled the right. They swung and grabbed at each other with such a ferocity it made Emma forget how comical it could seem. Then, to her horror, Mark's side bent over to pick up the knife and he stabbed it as hard as he could into Al's hand. Al screamed and Mark started stabbing the right side of their body in places that would cause maximum pain while inflicting minimal damage. This strategy proved effective, as the strength in Al's side of the body began to give way. The entire right side of the body slumped over, as if Al's spirit had been drained out of it. Mark's spirit took control and jumped up victorious.

Emma watched in horror as the psychopathic spirit possessing Al's body smiled wickedly and—to her disgust—licked some of Al's blood off the knife's blade.

"Now we can finish this," he grinned.

Once again he lifted the knife into the air, but before he could bring it down, the body he possessed began to shake as if it were a volcano nearing an eruption.

"What are you doing to me?" Mark's spirit cried out.

As an answer to his question, the body he was in exploded in a starburst of white-hot light. It blinded Emma for a moment and when she could finally see again, she saw a bloody and battered Al standing in front of an ethereal Mark.

"And stay out!" Al shouted at the insane phantom.

"You can't do this to me! I am the Phaetaboi!" Mark's spirit screamed back at him.

Al just shook his head. "Dude," he said to him, "you're no Phaetaboi. You're just one crazy dead fetaboy."

Mark's spirit screamed and threw itself into Al, but instead of possessing him all it did was bounce off of him as if it had hit a solid wall.

"You're not allowed in here anymore," Al told the now impotent spirit, "and you're not welcome in this restaurant anymore. If I hear anything about you trying to harm this woman, I will make you suffer."

"Your threats are meaningless!" Mark's spirit yelled at him. "You can't do anything to me!"

Al moved a step closer to the floating wraith and stared right into its dead eyes. "Why don't you try something and find out?"

Mark's spirit clenched its fists and threw them up in the air and screamed with a venomous hatred as it faded out of sight.

Al smiled, dropped the knife that was still in his hand and fell to the floor with a hard and painful thud. With the last of his strength he untied Emma's hands. She jumped up, ripped off her gag and ran out of the changing room shouting for help.

Much to the disbelief of George and his wife, an ambulance came to their restaurant for the third time in a week. Al went to the hospital, where his wounds were bandaged. It took him about a month to recover and when he came back to work he asked George if it was all right for him to just stay in the dish pit from that point on.

"It's safer in there," he explained.

George understood what he meant.

An Island Memory

The storm came out of nowhere. Robert and David had been sleeping in the small hold of their boat when the sound of the thunder and the violent rocking of the waves almost tossed them out of their cots. Bleary-eyed, they threw their raincoats over the underwear they slept in and went up on deck, where they were pelted by a rain so ferocious that a single droplet felt like a hurled rock.

As bad as the storm was, it was not enough to frighten the two brothers, who in the course of their year-long voyage had managed to endure much worse. They had seen enough by now to know that they weren't in any great danger and that for the moment the ship was safe, so they tightened a few knots, double-checked their equipment and then went back into the hold, grateful to get away from the hateful rain.

They flipped a coin to see who would go to sleep while the other stayed awake in case the situation suddenly turned for the worse. Robert won. He settled down onto his cot and almost instantly fell asleep, being the type of person who could nap in any situation. David picked up a magazine devoted to airplanes that he had bought at the last port. He had already read all the articles four times, but he still liked to look at the pictures of the different planes. Even though he had spent the past 10 months on a boat, flying was his real passion. He had gotten his first pilot's license when he was 17 and had managed to upgrade it several times over the past 10 years. Before he left to travel with

Robert, he had seriously considered trying to get a job as a commercial pilot, but he had been dissuaded by a friend who worked at a major airline and warned him about the low pay and long hours. David didn't need the money, since his family was wealthy, but the time when being an airline pilot automatically brought you respect and admiration had passed, and he thought it was better just to fly as a hobby.

As he flipped through the magazine, his eyelids began to grow heavy, so he grabbed a cola out of their small fridge and popped it open, hoping its caffeine would help keep him awake. He was sipping from the can when he simultaneously heard a crack of thunder and felt a sudden flash of heat. He jumped up and dropped the magazine and soda. Robert snapped out of his sleep and sat up. Even he couldn't sleep through what had just happened.

Without even throwing on their raincoats, they ran on deck and saw that the bolt of lightning that had just hit them had blackened the deck. The hard rain had kept the fire from growing, which was a relief, but their sail had been destroyed and in the darkness they could see debris that still glowed red from the heat.

"Do you know how lucky we are?" Robert shouted over the roar of the storm. "If we had any gasoline or propane on board, we'd be dead now."

David nodded. He grabbed an oar and used it to pick up some dying embers and throw them over the edge, while his brother inspected the damage. The rain grew harder and the waves more violent. It became difficult for them to stand as the boat rocked and the wind and rain raged against them. David was knocked off his feet and he fell painfully against the deck. He heard something snap and felt a tremendous jolt of excruciating pain surge through his right arm. He looked up at his brother and was horrified to see that in front of them was the single biggest wave he had ever seen in his life.

"Robert!" he shouted, but before he could warn his brother, the wave hit them.

* * *

David tried to sleep, but even his exhaustion wasn't enough to earn him some much-needed rest. The sun still blazed above him and when he opened his eyes he had to use his left hand to shade them from its blinding rays. A combination of starvation and dehydration kept him in a state of hazy consciousness. His body was so tired, he found it difficult to stay awake, but thanks to his hunger, pain and now-constant thirst, he couldn't fall asleep.

He had no memory of what had happened after the wave hit the boat. All he remembered was waking up in a small rubber raft, adrift in the middle of the ocean. He had no idea what had happened to his brother or their boat. He didn't know how he had gotten into the raft, and he didn't know how long he had been unconscious. One of the few things he did know was that he had been in the raft for close to two and a half days since he first awoke and that he no longer dreamed of being rescued. Instead he dreamed of rolling out of the raft and drinking in the salt water that surrounded him until he drowned. It was only the most primal of survival instincts that kept him from making this dream of suicide a reality.

He tried to think of happy times, when pain wasn't the only constant in his life, but these thoughts were constantly interrupted by the gnawing emptiness in his stomach, the painful dryness of his swallows, the jabbing pain in his arm and the molten throb of his sunburned skin. The only thing that managed to dull the edge of the pain was to dream of his time spent in the air. He dreamed of the tranquility of soaring through the air in a glider, when he most truly felt like a bird in the sky, and he dreamed of the time he got the chance to sit in the back of an F-16, when he most truly felt like a god in control of the universe.

It didn't take long for him to become so weak that he couldn't even raise his head. All he could see were the rubber edges of his floating prison. By now, even if by some miracle someone passed by him, he had no way to see them or get their attention. Lying there, he accepted his fate and waited for death to come. He closed his eyes and hoped it would come quickly.

As he waited, he heard a splashing sound in the distance. Over what seemed like an hour—but could have been just a few minutes—it grew closer and closer until it was right beside him. He assumed that he was imagining it and kept quiet. But then he felt the raft move more quickly than it had before, as if it was being pulled by someone. For the first time that day, he managed to speak.

"Is someone there?" His voice was nothing but a painful rasp, but it was loud enough to be heard.

"Yes," a voice answered and the raft continued to move along.

Over the next week, David drifted in and out of consciousness. During his more lucid moments he found himself in a cool dark space, lit by a handful of primitive torches. His right arm was encased in a makeshift splint made out of bark, leaves and vine. A wet fabric placed over his body helped to ease the pain of his burned skin, and someone kept making him drink cupful after cupful of cool fresh water. The space was too dimly lit for him to make the figure out, but the voice that spoke to him was definitely feminine.

"I'm sorry," she apologized to him once as she fed him something that tasted like a fishy broth, "but I've never done this before. For all I know, I'm only making you worse."

Her worries, though, turned out to be unfounded, as David eventually began to recover. He was soon well enough to ask his gracious host who she was and where they were.

"You can call me Amy," the woman told him, "and we're on an island somewhere between Hawaii and Australia. Beyond that, I don't have a clue."

"How long have you been here?" asked David.

"To tell you the truth, I've lost track. I tried to count the days when I first got here, but eventually I had to stop when it began to depress me. It's been years, though, I know that much."

David then tried to ask her how she'd ended up on the island, but before he could finish his question, she told him to be quiet and get some rest. He was tired, so he listened to her, but the question still lingered in his brain as he went to sleep.

By the end of that week, David was judged well enough to get up and leave the cave. His muscles ached and his body felt heavier than it ever had before, but he managed—with Amy's help—to stand up and walk out into the sunlight.

The island was like something out of a movie. The center was thickly forested with tall palm trees and long vines, surrounded by a sandy white beach and crystal blue water. Amy showed him around and told him that besides some shellfish at the beach, the two of them were pretty much it for wildlife.

"We're the only mammals here, so I hope you like seafood."

She then showed him the small pond that was the source of their fresh water.

"It looks pretty pathetic now," she admitted, "but it fills up whenever it rains, which it does fairly often."

After almost three weeks inside the dimly lit cave, this excursion outside allowed David his first opportunity to get a real look at Amy, who had previously existed in his mind only as a vaguely feminine, benevolent shape. Now he could see that she was older than he was, by about five to ten years. Her long ragged hair was ostensibly brown, but years in the sunlight had streaked it with natural blonde highlights. Her face was attractive, without being pretty. Her skin was darkly tanned, and her clothes were ragged and cut up. Years of surviving alone on the island had made her strong and muscular. Looking at her, David was struck by two thoughts. The first was "I have never seen anyone like this before," and the second was "she looks familiar."

They stayed outside for an hour before David asked to go back to the cave. His legs ached and it was becoming difficult for him to remain upright. Amy helped him back and together they sat in the cave and talked. Or more accurately, David talked and Amy listened. He told her all he knew about how he had ended up on a raft floating aimlessly in the middle of an ocean and about his family and what he did back home.

David watched Amy as she sat and listened to him. It soon became obvious to him that over the time she had been stranded on the island she had become so desperate for companionship that she would have been equally enthralled if he had read aloud from a phone book. She took everything in as if he was telling the most exciting story ever devised in the history of the world. She said little, only occasionally prodding him to continue or asking little questions to help him along, but when he started talking about how much he loved to fly she virtually exploded with delight.

"You're a pilot?" she asked him, her face flushed with excitement.

"Yeah," he grinned sheepishly, taken aback by her sudden burst of enthusiasm.

"What do you fly?"

"Anything I can get my hands on, really."

He then described all the types of aircraft he had either flown himself or sat in as a passenger. As he talked, a look of stunned amazement took hold of Amy's face. She made him go over every detail of his different flights, and she shook her head in awe as he talked about what it felt like to fly in a jet, literally faster than a bullet, and the joy he felt flying alone in a single-engine two-seater.

The questions she asked and the speed with which she threw them at him quickly made it clear that Amy also knew something about flying.

"You must be a pilot," he laughed when she asked him another difficult technical question.

She smiled at this. "It's been awhile," she admitted.

Months passed and David slowly got better. Soon he was able to leave the cave by himself and explore the small island that was now his home. Amy taught him the routine that she had developed over the years, and he adapted to it quickly. He grew to really like Amy, although he was sometimes annoyed by her refusal to talk about herself and wished that she would tell him more about how she'd ended up on the island.

But she wasn't the only mystery on the island. One morning David was walking back from the pond—or puddle, as they had taken to calling it—when he noticed that a bush he had walked past a hundred times appeared to be blocking the entrance to another cave. Curious, he snapped off some branches and stuck his head into the opening. He couldn't see anything, but he wondered why Amy hadn't set up camp in there, given how much closer it was to their only source of fresh water.

He asked her this when he found her at the beach, grabbing some crabs for dinner.

She stopped what she was doing and frowned. "Don't go in there," she warned him. "It's not safe."

"Why? What's in there?"

For a moment it seemed that she wanted to tell him, but she stopped herself and shook her head. "It's better if you don't know."

David lost his patience. "Damn it, Amy," he cursed at her, "I'm tired of all your secrets. What are you protecting me from? Whatever it is can't be worse than being stranded on a deserted island."

She waited for him to calm down before she said anything.

"I can't tell you," she said as kindly as she could. "I want to, but I can't. You are just going to have to trust me. Now promise me that you will stay out of that cave."

David didn't say anything for a moment.

"All right," he finally said. "I promise."

When David was 10 years old he saw his father dress up like a clown and spend the day sitting in one of those tanks where people throw baseballs at the target in the hopes of dunking the unfortunate person inside. The water was cold and his dad got dunked into it many times over the course of the day. He did not look as if he was having fun. When they drove home David asked his father why he had done it.

"Because it was for charity," his father answered.

David thought about this.

"But," he continued, unsatisfied with this answer, "couldn't you have just donated some money instead?"

"I could have," his father admitted, "but Reverend Gacy asked me to sit in the tank and I promised him I would."

"But you looked so miserable."

"Well, it wasn't very much fun."

"So why didn't you quit? You could have just gotten out and wrote a check, right?"

His father nodded. "Yes, I could have done that, but I didn't because I gave my word that I would take part for the whole day."

"I don't get it."

David's father turned the car off the road and stopped it. He turned towards his son and spoke to him.

"David," he said, "a man is only as good as his word. If you make a promise to someone then you have to keep it, even if it means doing something you don't like—*especially* if it means doing something you don't like. If someone asks you to do something and you have no intention of doing it, then say that you won't do it, because in this world there is no one worse than someone who breaks a promise."

It was because of those words and the effect they had had on David that over the course of his next seven years on the island, he never once went into the cave by the pond. He thought about it—a lot—but he never went inside.

For the first couple of years, David had cut his hair and trimmed his beard using the one knife Amy had, but after a while he decided that if he was going to live like

Robinson Crusoe, then he might as well look the part. He let his hair grow long and stopped worrying about his beard. Now when he checked out his reflection in the water he could barely recognize the man he saw looking back at him.

"I look like one of those guys who used to sell pottery at Grateful Dead concerts," he joked to Amy once. She didn't get it, but then she almost never did. "Aw, c'mon," he sighed, "you've had to have heard of the Grateful Dead."

"Sorry," she shrugged.

Once when he received a similar blank look after making a comment about the Beatles, all he could do was stare at her dumbfounded.

"You know," he told her, "sometimes I think that before you became stranded on a deserted island you were stranded on a deserted island."

One night, during their sixth year together, David and Amy sat at their beach and looked out into the ocean as the sun set behind them. David looked at her and noticed something.

"What?" she asked him when she caught him looking at her.

"You know what?" he asked her. "You look almost exactly the same as you did when I first met you. You haven't aged a day."

She smiled. "Diet and exercise," she told him. "Diet and exercise."

Once Amy asked David if he was lonely.

"I'm all right," he told her, "as long as you're around."

She smiled, but that wasn't the answer that she wanted. "That's not what I meant."

It took David a second to understand. "Oh," he said when he got it. "Sometimes."

"You don't have to be."

David looked at her and thought about what she said.

"No," he said finally, "I'm okay. Everything's okay. I like it how it is."

Amy threw an arm around his shoulder and gave him half a hug.

"Me, too," she smiled.

For a long time David thought about nothing but being rescued. He spent days and months devising ways to capture the attention of passing boats or planes, but all his efforts were thwarted because boats and planes never passed by the island. Eventually he abandoned the idea of ever leaving the island and focused on enjoying life where he was. He lived happily like this for several years, until one morning he got up and walked to the beach and saw a large ship in the distance. Tears came to his eyes as he began to scream and shout. He ran back to the cave and told Amy what he'd seen.

"We have to do something!" he insisted. "We have to get their attention."

He was too excited to notice that Amy wasn't as thrilled as she should have been and that the smile on her face was bittersweet. While he paced back and forth and tried to devise some sort of plan, she walked into their cave and found a box. She walked back out and handed it to him.

"There are flares in here," she told him, "but they are very old. There is a good chance that they won't work."

David opened the box and saw that it contained a flare gun and four flares. He shouted and laughed and hugged Amy and kissed her on the lips.

"We're going home!" he told her.

She didn't say anything.

David turned around and ran to the beach as fast as he could. He loaded a flare into the gun and pointed it into the air and pulled the trigger. Nothing happened. He swore loudly and threw the dud flare out of the gun and loaded another one from the box. He held the gun up and pulled the trigger and again nothing happened.

"Don't do this to me!" he shouted as he dumped the second dud out of the gun.

He loaded the third flare, held the gun up in the air and pulled the trigger. Tears of frustration overcame him when it too proved worthless.

"I told you," Amy said quietly behind him, "they're very old."

David looked down into the box and saw that there was just one left.

"Please," he whispered, "please."

He picked up the last flare and loaded it into the gun. He was so afraid that it was another dud that he almost preferred the idea of not pulling the trigger and finding out, but finally he found the courage to raise the gun and fire.

The flare shot out of the gun and flew into the sky. A trail of smoke followed it as arced above them and headed towards the ocean.

"See it," David pleaded, "please let someone see it!"

Soon the flare began to fall.

"That's not long enough!" David shouted helplessly. "They couldn't have seen that."

All at once the will to stand ebbed out of him and he fell backwards onto the sand. He buried his face into his hands and began to weep. For the first time since he had been alone at sea dying in his yellow rubber raft, he wished that he were dead.

"David!" Amy shouted behind him. "Look!"

David uncovered his eyes and in the distance saw a flare fly through the air. It had come from the ship.

He screamed with joy and ran to Amy and hugged her while he jumped up and down.

"We did it!" he shouted. "We're going home!"

Amy let him enjoy his celebration before she finally spoke.

"David," she said softly, "I have something to tell you."

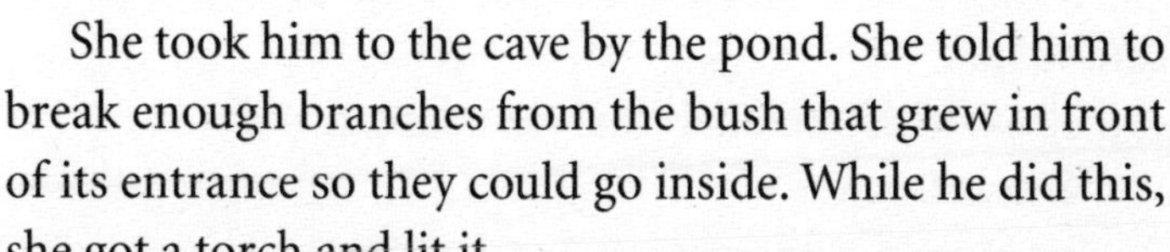

She took him to the cave by the pond. She told him to break enough branches from the bush that grew in front of its entrance so they could go inside. While he did this, she got a torch and lit it.

The first thing David had noticed was that this cave was bigger than the one they lived in. He followed her as she walked and stopped when she crouched down beside something. In the darkness, with just the torch to see everything, he could barely make out what it was.

"Is that—" he asked.

"Yes, it is."

"Do you—" He crouched down with her. "Do you know whose it is?"

She nodded. "David," she said to him, "it's mine."

He didn't understand. He looked down at the skeleton in front of him and tried to comprehend what she had just said.

"What?" was the best he could manage.

"That's me," Amy explained. "This is where I died."

With that said, she stood up and handed him the torch before walking out of the cave. He stayed where he was and examined what he found around him. The cave was littered with different possessions. One of the first things he grabbed was a book that lay on the floor. He could tell that it was a journal but years inside a damp cave had reduced most of its words to illegible blotches. Fortunately, the name written on the inside of the front cover was still intact. David closed his eyes after he read it. At that moment he knew everything and nothing all at once. He got up and walked out of the cave. He found Amy standing in front of the pond.

"You never told me Amy was short for Amelia," he said to her.

"I haven't been called that for a long time."

"Over 60 years?"

She looked surprised.

"That's right. How did you know?"

"People have been wondering about what happened to you ever since you disappeared," he told her. His next words now seemed painfully intrusive, but he couldn't stop himself from asking them. "What did happen?"

She shrugged. "We ran out of fuel and had to make an emergency landing. I managed to bring it into the water without doing too much damage and the plane floated for a couple of minutes before it began to take on water. Fred and I grabbed everything we could and got into a life raft and floated around for what seemed like weeks." Amy paused for a moment while she remembered her old navigator. "He didn't make it. I'm not sure how I did. I was ready to die when I felt the raft hit dry land. Somehow I managed to get out and find this pond. I was so thirsty it hurt to drink from it, but it saved my life. Then I went over to that cave and I lived there alone for I don't know how long. That is until I started to feel this pain in my side. It was quick. I barely felt it, but when it was over I found myself standing over my body."

Just by looking at him, she could tell what he wanted to ask.

"I don't know why," she admitted. "I've had a long time to think about it now and the only thing I can come up with is that this island sat empty for thousands, maybe even millions of years. That's a long time to be alone, even if you're not really alive. So I think that when I arrived here, it got used to me. It liked having me around, but then I died." Amy struggled to find the words that she wanted. "I don't think I'm really here. I think I'm just someone the island remembers."

David didn't know what to say.

"They'll be here soon," she reminded him.

He nodded silently.

"David?" she asked quietly.

"Yeah?"

"Do you remember how we always complained that so few airplanes ever flew past us?"

"Yeah."

"Could you do me a favor?"

"Of course. Anything."

"Could you fly over here sometime? I don't care what kind of plane it is. Anything will do. I just want to see you fly." Her voice had remained steady, but tears misted her eyes.

David grabbed her and hugged her close to him.

"I promise," he whispered to her.

"Thank you," she whispered back.

He let her go. "You don't have to thank me," he insisted, "not after everything you've done for me."

They could hear the sounds of a group of men arriving on the island. They knew they had only a few seconds left together.

"David?" she asked again.

"Yeah?"

"I love you."

"I love you too."

"Good-bye."

"Good-bye."

They hugged one last time and then Amy turned around and began to walk away. David turned the other way and headed towards the beach.

Amy had forgotten all about the little things she had done to pass the time before David had saved her from her loneliness. It took her several months to take them up again, but now they seemed like what they were—empty pursuits that served little real purpose. After a while she abandoned them again and spent most of her time at the beach. She would lie in the sand and look up into the sky and wait.

The morning was sunny and bright. The sky above was as clear as she had ever seen it. She lay down on the warm sand and used her hands to shade her eyes from the sun.

A sound rumbled in the distance. She sat up and searched the sky around her. It took her a second, but then she found it. It flew towards her slowly, with the grace of an angel. She didn't recognize what kind it was, but that didn't matter.

She jumped up from the sand and began to cheer as it passed over her. She laughed and cried and jumped and clapped. Within five minutes it was out of sight again. Both giddy and exhausted, she sat back down on the sand, a smile on her face as wide as the ocean that surrounded her. She lay back down and thanked the world for remembered promises.

The Phantom and the Wraith

It was thanks to a bizarre coincidence that the NAHL hockey draft of 2001 got more news coverage than all the previous drafts combined. Despite the booming popularity of the North America Hockey League, the majority of this interest had nothing to do with the sport. Instead it centered on the history of its number one and two draft picks, Kyle Simmons and Brian Frampton. Considered by the experts to be two of the most promising players of all time, what made their spots at the top of the draft unique was that not only were they from the same small town of Beatty, Saskatchewan, but they had literally grown up beside each other as next-door neighbors.

For many this coincidence seemed straight out of a poorly written TV movie, but the one fact that added spice to the story and got it more print space than it may have deserved was that despite—or perhaps because of—their close proximity throughout their youth, Kyle and Brian loathed each other. Their rivalry was fueled by a pure mutual hatred, and what made their story sell so well were the insults and slanders that they lobbed at each other whenever they had the chance. But as fierce as they were off the ice, their words were nothing compared to the competitive fury that fired them when they played hockey against each other. Ever since they were old enough to play street hockey with the other neighborhood kids, their only goal was the complete and total humiliation of the other.

Many of the articles written about them tried to come up with an explanation for their antipathy, most suggesting it was just the result of professional jealousy. But those who really knew the two players found this assessment simplistic. Their hatred stemmed from some place deeper and more primal than normal envy or jealousy. They had been born with it.

Beyond their skill, the street where they grew up and their hatred for each other, the two young men had nothing in common. Physically, mentally and emotionally they were polar opposites.

Kyle, who would never let Brian forget that he was chosen as the number one draft pick by the Edmonton Maulers, was small for a hockey player. He was 5' 9", weighed 175 pounds and looked more like a high school English teacher than the top rookie in the league. He made up for his physical limitations with incredible speed, shooting accuracy and almost supernatural ability to be in exactly the right place on the ice at exactly the right time. It was because of the way he would suddenly appear out of nowhere to get the puck that he earned the nickname the Phantom. Well regarded for his sportsmanlike conduct, Kyle was a gentleman off the ice as well. Quiet, humble and unfailingly polite (except when he was talking to or about Brian), he was the type of player coaches and parents pointed to as a role model for their players and children.

The same could not be said for Brian. If anything he was the type of player that young disciples of the sport should do their best to avoid emulating. He was a showoff and a glory hog who took credit for every win and assigned blame to others for every loss. To look at him one would assume that he was a heavyweight boxer or a professional wrestler rather than a hockey player. He stood 6' 5" and weighed 295 pounds. Most men his size could barely hold themselves up on ice skates, but Brian was almost as fast as Kyle, though he lacked his former neighbor's on-ice sixth sense. He allowed his size and muscle to make up for this difference and got to where he had to go by plowing through whatever was in his path. It was because of his bone-jarring hits that he had earned the nickname the Wraith. To use the language of the sport, he was a goon, which was a title he had also earned in everyday life.

He had been drafted by the New York Liberties, and as the new season began, sports fans everywhere counted the days until he and Kyle finally met on the ice. It took two months, but it was worth the wait.

The Maulers and the Liberties played so fiercely that the game became legendary in the sports community. One sports writer suggested that it ranked up there with Muhammad Ali and Joe Frazier's "Thrilla in Manila" as a perfect example of two competitors summoning up superhuman endurance in order to prevail. And while the game was a team effort, everyone who watched it knew that Kyle and Brian were the only men on the ice who mattered. If in their famous battle, Ali and Frazier threw 300 punches that would kill an average man, Kyle and Brian equaled their feat by putting in an effort that would send the average hockey player to the hospital with exhaustion. As hard as they fought, though, in the end they had to settle for a tie. After an overtime so vicious that the referees gave up handing out penalties for fear of leaving no one in the game, the score was 6–6.

Kyle scored four times for the Maulers and assisted on their other two goals, which he felt gave him a small victory over his rival, who scored three times for the Liberties but whose selfish play meant he didn't make any assists.

As the season went on and the two teams met again, it became evident that their first encounter had been no fluke. Hockey fans everywhere prayed that the two teams would make it to the finals of the Kelly Cup, because they knew the result would be the most exciting and dramatic cup battle of all time.

Thanks to the efforts of Kyle and Brian, the fans' prayers came true. The Maulers and the Liberties trounced the other teams they faced in the playoffs so quickly that it seemed as though the hockey gods could not wait for them to get together. Knowing that this would be the most talked about and watched series of all time, the NAHL did their best to publicize their two most important players.

Someone high up in the organization decided that it would be a great story if Brian and Kyle made a pre-series trip to Beatty, where they would be honored by their proud hometown. Brian and Kyle were both reluctant to go on this trip. Neither wanted to spend the time it would take to go home when they could use it to practice, but both of their teams agreed with the league that it would be a waste not to grab the extra publicity and play up the extraordinary nature of the series. They pushed the two players to go and that was why—for the first time since they were teenagers—the two men found themselves sitting together.

The plane was small and uncomfortable. To make matters even worse, the weather changed dramatically over the course of their short flight. It had been warm and sunny when they had taken off, but shortly after take-off storm clouds had begun to form around them. Along with Brian and Kyle there was Carol Liebman, a small, efficient woman who worked as a publicity liaison for the league, and Edward Braddock, the pilot, an older man with salt-and-pepper hair and an unfortunate tendency to share anecdotes about his in-air near-death experiences.

"This is nothing," he laughed as a sudden burst of thunder caused Carol to jump in her seat beside him. "Three years ago I got caught in a storm that made this one seem like a cool spring shower. I was flying some ad executives to one of those business retreats when it just started coming down like it did when Noah finished his ark. We're talking *barrels* of water. I had zero visibility. I mean a 747 could've been heading straight towards me and I wouldn't have seen it, it was so bad—"

Kyle tried to ignore Edward by examining his fingernails. He looked down and saw that Brian was gripping his armrests so tightly that he seemed in danger of ripping them off the chair.

"Excuse me," he interrupted Edward, "but could you change the subject? You're making the big guy uncomfortable."

"Oh?" Edward sounded surprised. "I'm sorry."

Brian's face turned red. "I wasn't uncomfortable," he protested angrily.

"Uh-huh," Kyle grinned patronizingly.

"I wasn't!"

For a second Carol forgot about how scared she was as she sighed and crossed her arms. Since she had been with the two men they hadn't been able to exchange three words without starting some sort of argument.

"Hey, it takes a big man to admit he's scared," teased Kyle.

"You're the one who's scared!"

"Score another brilliant comeback for the behemoth."

"You're a behemoth!"

"No, I'm not. You'd know that if you actually picked up a book once in a while." Kyle paused before adding, "Not that you could actually read it if you did."

"Do you wanna go?" Brian seethed.

"Yes, Brian," Kyle retorted sarcastically, "I want to *go.* Do you want to do it right here inside the airplane or do you want to go outside?"

"Shut up!"

"Oh, how can I ever outwit you if you're going to keep coming up with these exquisite bons mots?"

"I tell you what, if you don't shut up I'll exquisite bon mot you right in the face."

"Stop it!" Carol shouted at them. "You're worse than children."

"He started it," Brian whined.

"I don't want to hear it," she snapped at them.

For the next few minutes they sat in silence before Edward decided it was the perfect time to talk about how he once had to make an emergency landing when a goose flew into his engine.

"Yeah, I was worried there for a second. Thought I'd bought the farm on that one. This is nothing. You guys have nothing to worry about."

* * *

When Carol's boyfriend, Connor, checked his answering machine that night he never expected that he would be the first person to hear the message that would end up being replayed on almost every news channel in the world. It was so full of static that it was hard to understand, but most experts agreed that under the circumstances it was a minor miracle that anything was heard at all.

It began with Carol.

"Connor? Connor?" she sobbed. "If you're there, then pick up. I have to speak to someone. We're going down and we might not make it. This idiot flying the plane—"

"Hey!" protested a voice in the background.

"—keeps saying that we're going to be fine, but just in case I want to tell you that I love you and that I'm sorry about the thing with Kenny. I'm sorry about everything. Tell my parents that I love them and that I would have called them but they were too far away…"

Carol continued to speak, but in all the newscasts her voice was drowned out by what was being said behind her.

"This is all your fault!" accused Brian.

"How is this my fault?" protested Kyle.

"Shut up!"

"I can't believe it. I'm going to die and my last conversation is going to be with the stupidest man on earth."

"You better hope you die, 'cause if we get out of this alive I'm going to kill you during the playoffs."

Kyle snorted. "That *would* be the only way you could win."

"Shut up!"

Those were the last words heard in the message before it descended into a horrible and agonizing silence.

It took 10 hours after Connor reported hearing the tape for the plane to be found. The authorities quickly concluded that everyone inside had died on impact. It didn't take long for a rumor to take hold that the bodies of the two famous passengers were found with their hands wrapped around each other's throats, but this was never verified and was widely denounced as ridiculous by everyone involved in the investigation of the crash.

There was talk after the plane crash of the possibility that the final series between the Maulers and the Liberties would be canceled. Some people believed that to play for the cup so soon after the tragedy would be distasteful and disrespectful, but they were in the minority. The NAHL took a poll and found that 87% of season-ticket holders agreed that the two departed players would want the games to be played. As a compromise, the league postponed the series for three weeks, during which they aired a run of TV spots honoring Brian and Kyle.

When it came time for the series to start, the general feeling was one of ambivalence. The excitement that had been sparked by the famous rivalry was gone and in its place all that was left was a feeling of lackluster obligation. Since the purpose of the series now seemed to be both to win the cup and to honor a fallen teammate, virtually everyone believed that the Maulers would win easily in a four-game sweep. The Maulers were not necessarily the better team, but they actually liked the teammate they were playing for. It was no secret that when Brian died he had left no friends in the locker room, and it was hard to imagine the Liberties going the extra distance for someone they couldn't stand, no matter how good a hockey player he had been.

It came, then, as something of a shock when the Liberties beat the Maulers three games in a row.

The games were all close—each decided in overtime—but even so, there was something suspicious about the Liberties victories. Though they couldn't explain why, everyone agreed that something fishy was going on.

For all three of the games it was obvious that the Liberties were being completely outclassed by the Maulers. The Maulers were moving faster, passing better and taking advantage of all their scoring opportunities, while their opponents seemed to be more lackadaisical and slower to approach the net. Yet whenever the Maulers scored a well-deserved goal, the Liberties would score one of their own within two or three minutes. The rational explanation would be to blame the Maulers for lazy defense and goaltending, but no one who watched the games could provide any evidence of these problems occurring. The Liberties goals just *happened*, as if some otherworldly force was willing them. This aura of supernatural intervention was felt most during the third game's sudden-death overtime.

Despite the way the Maulers had dominated the Liberties throughout the first three periods, they still only managed to tie the game at a score of 2–2. The problem was that for some reason they couldn't make it to the net. Every time someone from the team managed to break through the Liberties offense and skate towards the goal, something inexplicable would happen to him. In the case of Edrick LeFay, the screws in his left skate fell out, causing him to topple as the blade came loose. For Denis L'Ange, the problem came when the visor on his helmet suddenly steamed up and made it impossible for him to see. But the most bizarre of all the incidents happened to Sherman Roy during the first minute of overtime. A fast skater with impressive accuracy, he was barreling towards the goal with the puck when—in front of everyone in the stadium and the millions watching on television—he ran into an invisible wall. He hit it with such a force that it caused him to fly off his feet and land painfully on his back. The resulting injury to his spine was so severe it seemed unlikely that he would be able to play for most of the next season, much less the next game. After he was carried off the ice, the Maulers were still so bewildered by what they had seen that the Liberties were able to sneak a goal in and win the game.

No one wanted to say the word *ghost.* They were all thinking it, but no one wanted to be the crazy person who suggested it. Some fans, however, alluded to the possibility as they sat drinking in their favorite sports bars.

"I tell ya," one fan expounded to his friend, "that Frampton guy was a *monster.* He was huge! Anybody who tried to skate into him wouldn't get up for a long time, I'll tell you that!"

"But he's dead," his friend reminded him.

"Who said he wasn't?" the man answered.

But despite the reluctance of all those watching to admit that something supernatural was going on, word began to spread and as a result the fourth game in the series became the most watched in the league's history. Everyone wanted to see whether—in what could be a deciding game—things got even more unusual.

They certainly did, but not in the way people expected.

With everything on the line for them, something happened to the Maulers. It was as though wings had grown on their feet and eyes had grown out of the backs of their heads. They skated so fast and passed so well it was almost superhuman. They themselves looked shocked as they scored goal after goal. Just as in the previous games, the Liberties seemed to be aided by some brute invisible force, but now a more powerful and elegant spirit in support of the team from Edmonton was counteracting it. Now the Maulers found themselves suddenly stopping before they ran into one of those invisible barriers that had crippled Sherman, and they managed to get off the ice before a piece of their equipment started to fall apart. Thanks to this newly developed sixth sense they were able to finally beat the Liberties 7–2.

It was clear to everyone who watched the game that night what had happened. No one directly talked about it, but they all knew how the Maulers had finally gotten their edge back. The debate between the fans remained as oblique as ever, but the focus had definitely changed.

"I tell ya," one fan expounded to his friend, "that Simmons guy was an *artist.* He was amazing! Anybody who tried to out-finesse him was sure to lose, I tell you that!"

"But he's dead," his friend reminded him.

"Who said he wasn't?" the man answered.

The fifth game of the series was a near duplicate of the fourth with the Maulers beating the Liberties 6–3. But their fire faded during the sixth game and they barely managed to eke out a win in overtime. It appeared to everyone watching that the seventh and final game would be exactly what they first dreamed it would be—one of the closest and hardest-fought battles in Kelly Cup history. The sense of anticipation that overtook the fans was almost exactly like the feeling when the two teams had first met during the regular season. The only difference now was the supposed absence of the two players who had originally been responsible for the fans' high expectations. But now, at last, those fans were willing to admit what they had denied when the series had first started—that Kyle Simmons and Brian Frampton, the Phantom and the Wraith, were still very much in the game.

Before the game, the teams gathered in their respective locker rooms as their coaches led them in a prayer. What made the occasion unique was whom they were praying to.

Jean LeRue, the coach of the Liberties, closed his eyes as he spoke.

"Brian," he said, "we need your strength tonight. We need you to be our wall. Don't let them get past you. They are small and fast and tricky, but that is no match for your power. We ask you to help us smash them down and crush them into little pieces. Win this for us, Brian! Win this and your memory will never be forgotten!"

"Amen!" a few impassioned players shouted out.

Walter Kowalsky, the coach for the Maulers, spoke slowly and with great care.

"Kyle," he said, "you know what we are up against. They are strong, they are big and they are mean, but we are better. With your help, we can easily skate circles around them. Help us fly tonight. Help us aim tonight. Lead us to where we have to be tonight, and we guarantee that you will always be remembered as the better man."

The Maulers nodded silently at this, while they each individually asked Kyle for his help.

The final game was being played in Edmonton, and the fans assembled had high hopes for the game they were going to see that night. They couldn't have imagined what would actually occur.

It began right from the first face-off.

The Maulers' Edrick LeFay and the Liberties' Gary Dombroski stared each other down at center ice. The ref dropped the puck and LeFay felt what seemed like a brick wall hit him in the chest. He reeled and fell on his back, but before Dombroski could capitalize on this, the puck flew out of the center towards the Maulers' Miroslav Yanov, who skated with it towards the Liberties' net. Normally a fast skater, on this day Miroslav seemed to literally fly across the ice. A freeze-frame analysis would later prove that his blades were not touching the ice. He sailed towards the net and flipped the puck past the stunned goaltender.

A few minutes later the Liberties tied the game when the Maulers found themselves all tripping face first into the ice, as if some invisible hockey stick had been placed in front of their feet.

At the end of the first period the game was tied 3–3. The Liberties were exhausted from trying to keep up with the Maulers, and the Maulers were battered and bruised from the hits—both natural and supernatural—they were taking from the Liberties. The coaches for both teams tried to give their players a rousing pep talk, but everyone knew that they were all just pawns in a game none of them could control, and at this point all they really cared about was surviving it.

In the second period two players from the Maulers were removed from the ice in stretchers and one of the Liberties had to be treated for exhaustion. Despite an ever-escalating series of unearthly occurrences, the score didn't change.

The fans were uncharacteristically quiet. The thrill of seeing their team so close to winning the Kelly Cup was not enough to rouse them out of the stupor caused by witnessing not just one, but many miracles in succession. But the people who had it the worst were the officials, who found it almost impossible to keep order in a game where the two players responsible for most of the penalties had been dead for weeks.

Just like the second period, the third proved to be a washout. The game was still tied and ready to go into overtime, but almost no one on either team had the strength to stand, much less play until one of the teams scored. When play commenced the players on the ice looked as if they were 80 years old and had been playing for two days straight. But somehow the puck still managed to zing about the ice at furious speeds as the two ghosts gave up all pretense of playing through their teammates. During a Mauler line change, one of the players felt himself held back as a less physically substantial player took his spot on the ice.

The fans all saw this new player take shape in front of them as if he were a light connected to a dimmer switch, and his presence served as a splash of ice water to wake them from their virtual catatonia. Everyone in the stadium recognized him immediately.

"Simmons. Simmons. Simmons. Simmons..." they began to chant.

Kyle's spirit paid no attention to their cheers as his focus was directed on the ice.

The crowd knew it was only a matter of time before he was joined on the ice by his famed rival. All it took was the next Liberties line change for that to happen. The fans got to their feet when they saw the hulking specter appear, because now they knew the game would truly be decided. Brian's angry-looking spirit headed straight for Kyle's more focused apparition and a collision seemed inevitable, but just as Brian was about to crush the smaller man into the boards, Kyle moved away and left the behemoth with nothing to slam into but plastic.

Kyle's spirit easily stole the puck from a Liberties defenseman and he skated straight towards the Liberties net. Brian's spirit chased after him as fast as he could.

"Simmons. Simmons. Simmons. Simmons..." the crowd continued to chant.

Cameron Walters, the Liberties goaltender, started to shake as he watched two dead men hurtle towards him at a breakneck speed. Despite the great shivering terror that had taken hold of him, he tried to keep his eyes on the puck as Kyle's spirit moved right in front of him. He saw Kyle's ghost lift up his stick to take a shot and watched as it came down. He also saw Brian's ghost slam into Kyle so hard the stadium actually seemed to shake. Their impact was so violent that the resulting sudden flash of light temporarily blinded everyone who saw it. Cameron knew the puck was coming towards him, but he could not see and had to simply guess at its unearthly trajectory.

Everyone in the stadium blinked and got their vision back. They looked out to the Liberties net and screamed with cheers of joy when they saw the black puck behind the goal line.

The Maulers had won.

Things returned to normal after that.

There was some talk from the Liberties camp that the whole series should be replayed on account of paranormal interference, but the league's rules did not allow for this and the New York team was forced to accept its loss.

In Edmonton a huge parade was held to celebrate the victory and one car that drove in it was kept empty of passengers as a tribute to the player who made all the difference.

Whatever happened to Kyle's and Brian's spirits when they collided appeared to be permanent, as the two ghosts were never heard from again. As it happened, the same two teams made it to the Kelly Cup final the next year and without any supernatural aid the Maulers won it a second time in a four-game sweep. And the truth was that, as strange and exciting as the infamous battle between the two ghostly rivals had been, everyone agreed that this more conventional series was much more satisfying.

With Her Face in His Hands

Josiah had been retired for only a week when his doctor told him that he was going blind and that nothing could be done about it.

"Well," Josiah said, "at least I got the time for it."

There was no way to know exactly when his vision would fail him completely, but by his doctor's best estimates Josiah had six months to a year before he needed a dog and white cane.

Not being the type to trust doctors, Josiah decided to give himself just four months to prepare for that eventuality. During those months he learned how to read Braille and he walked around his neighborhood and the places where he hung out and memorized every step and turn and crack until he could literally walk them blindfolded. He bought himself a white cane and painted it purple so it had more style, and he began the process of getting a guide dog—a prospect that made him feel as excited as he had felt when his mama brought home Tin-Ear for his seventh birthday. He had never had time before to take care of a dog at home, but now that he did he looked forward to sharing his small bungalow.

During those four months he also made sure that his small castle was in as perfect condition as it could be, knowing that these would be the last repairs he would be able to make himself. He was proud of his house. It was the one he had been raised in, only then it was more of a shack than the comfortable home it was today. When his mama died, she left it to him because that was all she had to leave, and over the years he had worked on it and rebuilt it until it was easily the nicest house in the neighborhood. Everyone thought so.

The four months passed, and he could still see a little. He could tell, though, that he had only a few months left, so he settled into a routine, knowing that he would have to depend on it if he was going to continue being the man he always had been.

To look at him, one would not think of him as the retiring type. He looked 10 years younger than his actual age, and he seemed a little too energetic to be even that, but when you work as a firefighter there comes a time when you know you have to quit—and he knew, so he did.

He didn't have a wife. He had had a lot of girlfriends over the years, but he always seemed to be looking for something that he couldn't find and he was never able to commit himself to a woman the way he did to his work. He loved being a firefighter. If you asked him to tell you why, the words would come out slowly and clumsily, because it was hard for him to articulate just how much it meant to him to know that by just doing his job he was helping people. To know that just by waking up in the morning he was making a difference.

It had been hard when he started. He wasn't the first black man to work a truck in Denby, but the last one who did had worked in the 1920s. When he joined in 1969, when he was 24 and just out of the army, the South was still a very angry place to be. He had to work 10 times as hard as everyone else to prove that he belonged, and he had to deal with his share of idiotic comments and moronic slurs, but such was his devotion and intensity that many of the same men who had made his life so hard in the beginning were the ones who hugged him the hardest when he left.

His world was a full month away from being in total darkness when he heard about a community center a few miles from his house. People in his condition were known to gather at the center and play games and pass the time. Curious to find out what it was like, and eager not to burden his buddies by making them spend time with a blind man, he went to check it out. He got there by taking the bus, which stopped just a few steps away from his house. He never did like taking the bus, always having been the type of man who needed to be in control of any vehicle he was in, but he now had no option and he got used to it.

It turned out that the community center was a lot of fun. He met several people there he liked—like Joe, the old Italian barber who'd lost his sight when he was shot during a holdup, and Malcolm, a young man in his 20s who had been blinded by his mother when he was six. Josiah decided to make the place his new regular hangout, and he spent a few hours there almost every day.

The months went by quickly. Josiah got used to the darkness, and he immediately fell in love with Naomi, the German shepherd who became his guide dog. He also learned to become more attuned to the information that came to him through his nose and his ears. Soon he smelled things in the air he had never noticed before and was hearing noises he had never been aware of. Now when he met a woman, he remembered her not by her face and the way she wore her hair, but by how she smelled and the sound of her voice. He tried to learn how to picture people's faces by touching them with his hands, but he found he couldn't make the connection in his mind between how something felt and what it should look like. It also made him feel uncomfortable to do something so intimate with someone he'd just met. He had always been old-fashioned when it came to that sort of thing.

He had been blind for a year and a half on the sweet-smelling summer day he met Lucille. It was 10:30 in the morning and he and Naomi were on their way to the community center when he sat down at the bus stop. He had been sitting for only a minute when he noticed the scent of lilacs and perspiration, a not-unpleasant combination of perfume and the day's heat.

"Excuse me…" he said to the person from whom the flowery odor emanated.

There was no response, but to Josiah silence read as consent so he continued. "I was wondering if you could tell me when you see the number nine coming down the street? It would save me the bother of asking every driver who stops here if I'm on the right bus."

A young woman answered. Her voice was quiet and respectful. "Yes, sir."

"Thank you very much."

"You're welcome."

They didn't say anything else to each other until, about 12 minutes later, she told him that the number nine was coming down the street. He smiled, got up and waited for the sounds of the bus stopping and the doors opening. When he heard them, he let Naomi lead him up the steps of the bus, and he turned his head and thanked the woman again.

The next day when he arrived at the bus stop he noticed the same scent in the air as he sat down. As he did, he heard a voice speak to him.

"Are you still catching the number nine?"

"Yes, ma'am," he smiled.

"Okay."

They kept quiet until she told him that his bus was arriving and he thanked her, to which she replied with a quiet "you're welcome."

A slight head cold kept him from visiting the community center for the next three days, more because he didn't want to infect anybody than out of any personal discomfort. After several warm baths and a good deal of sleep he was feeling better and ready to go.

When he arrived at the bus stop he was pleasantly surprised to smell lilacs in the air.

"Hello," he greeted the young woman.

"Hello," she politely greeted him back.

"Nice day, isn't it?"

"Yes, sir. Very nice."

A few minutes passed before she spoke again.

"Your dog is very pretty."

"That's what everyone says," he smiled, "but I have to take their word for it."

"What's his name?"

"Naomi. He's a she."

"That's a nice name. What made you choose it?"

"I didn't. They named her before I got her, but I like it. It seems to suit her. She's very ladylike."

"Your bus is coming."

"Thank you…" He waited for her to fill in his silence with her name.

"Lucille," she supplied.

"Thank you, Lucille. I'm Josiah. Josiah Lamont." He stuck out his hand and she shook it; her hand was cold and her grip was featherlight.

"Good-bye, Lucille," he said, and smiled as he stood up and got on the bus.

"Good-bye, Mr. Lamont."

As Josiah sat in his seat there was a smile on his face.

The next day he arrived at the bus stop earlier than usual.

"Hello, Mr. Lamont."

"Hello, Lucille. How are you today?"

"I'm all right. How's Naomi?"

"As happy as ever." He laughed and gave the cheerful dog a scratch behind her ear.

"Are you catching the number nine again?"

He shook his head. "No. Just thought I'd go for a walk, but an old man like me needs his rest so I thought I'd sit here for a spell."

"You're not old."

He laughed. "They say you're only as old as you feel and some days that makes me 80, I reckon."

"You don't look like any 80-year-old I know."

"True...true...I am a handsome devil."

Lucille giggled softly at this. "Is there a Mrs. Lamont, Mr. Lamont?"

"I'm afraid not."

"That's a shame."

"Maybe it is. I don't know. Sometimes I think I wouldn't have made as good a fireman with a wife."

"You were a fireman?" There was an equal mixture of awe and shock in her voice, which amused him.

"Yes, ma'am. Twenty-five years."

"No. You're fooling me." She sounded incredulous.

"Swear to the Lord."

"I never met a colored fireman before."

Josiah was taken slightly aback by this. He hadn't been called colored since he was in his 20s. Maybe it was something the kids were doing these days. Those rapper guys were always bringing back things from the past.

"Well, it's my pleasure to be your first."

They spent the next hour just sitting and talking and not once did it occur to him that Lucille never had to leave to get on a bus.

When he got back home he found himself half humming and half singing a song he hadn't thought about since he was a teenager. If it is true that you're only as old as you feel, then he was 18.

Over the next three weeks Josiah spent at least an hour every day at the bus stop talking to Lucille; they laughed and shared stories and for the first time ever he felt as though he had found what he had always been looking for.

"Josiah…" She still sounded uncomfortable using his first name, but he had insisted that she do so.

"Yes, ma'am?" It sounded as though she needed this permission to continue.

"Why did you become a fireman?"

Josiah was quiet for a while. "A pretty girl," he finally admitted.

"Truly?"

He nodded his head. He had never told this story before.

"In all my life I've never seen another woman as beautiful. Once some guys at the station brought in a video of that Flintstones movie, I don't know if you've seen it or not, and there was a woman in it who was close, but even then she was like a whisper and this other woman was like a hundred-person choir. I was 12 and my mama had sent me out to get some flour for the biscuits she was famous for. Whenever I went to the store I always spent a couple of minutes looking through the new comic books to find out how Superman and Batman were doing, and it was while I was reading one of those books that I saw her walk in."

The recollection kept him silent for a moment.

"Back then there weren't many strangers around here, so it was rare to see someone you'd never seen before. I watched her as she picked up a cola and paid for it at the counter. As she gave Mr. Thomas her change she asked him if he was going to be at the meeting at the local church. He said he wasn't and she told him that he really should go, that it was important. It wasn't until later that I found out she was with a group that was trying to organize a bus boycott like they did in Alabama after that woman was arrested for refusing to give up her seat."

"Rosa Parks." Lucille's voice became solemn.

"You've heard of her?"

"She's my hero."

"That's good. It's good that young people like you remember the past like that. So many kids have no idea about what it was like before. They think they're repressed now. I bet if you went down to the local high school most of the kids couldn't tell you who Rosa Parks is, and the only reason they know who Martin Luther King Jr. is, is because they have a holiday named after him."

"I don't know about you, Josiah. You say the strangest things sometimes."

"I know, I'm just a mean old man."

"What happened to the girl?"

"I followed her. I forgot all about the flour and followed her to the church where the meeting was being held. I was going to go in, when I realized how mad my mama was going to be if I didn't get back right away with what she wanted. So I ran to the store and got some flour and ran home. It was while I was running that I heard it. It…" Josiah struggled to find the words to describe the sound that echoed so loudly in his memories. "It was like thunder had started screaming" was the best that he could do. "I dropped the flour and ran towards it. I don't know why. I just had to. Even from blocks away I could feel the heat, and the smell…" Josiah remembered the horrible smell and he whispered, "No one survived. The fire took them all."

"And that's why?"

"Yes. That's why."

Uncomfortable with the melancholy his story had brought about, Josiah changed the subject. "Now it's my turn to ask you a question."

"I suppose it is at that."

"What's a young girl like you doing sitting at a bus stop with an old man like me?"

"I'm waiting for a bus."

"Are you sure it's coming?" he teased her.

"It should. Any second now. And when I get on it I'm not going to sit in the back, no matter what anybody says. I'm going to sit right in the front and when they tell me to move I'm not going to budge. They're going to have to take me to jail before I move one bit." Her voice was stronger and more determined than he had ever heard it before; it was filled with a passion he had seldom encountered.

He didn't understand what she was talking about. "Why would anybody tell you to move?"

"Because I'm colored."

"But buses haven't been segregated for years."

"Now stop being silly, Josiah," she chided him.

"I'm not." He wanted more than anything to be able to look at her face to see if she was just having fun with a blind man, but he had only her voice and it was as sincere as anything he had ever heard.

"Lucille..." It was now his turn to be bashful.

"Yes, Josiah?"

"Can I...can I put my hands on your face?"

"Why would you want to do that?"

"So I can find out what you look like."

There was a pause before she answered. "I guess that would be all right."

Slowly and carefully he raised his hands up and she guided them to her face. Her skin was soft and unblemished and cold to the touch. His hands moved up and down and for the first time his mind was able to see the face that he held. She was so beautiful that a hundred-person choir began to sing inside his head. Tears began to fall down his cheeks. It had been a long time since he had last cried, back when he was a young boy standing in front of a blazing monument to prejudice and hate. These tears were different. They were warm and comforting and with them that young boy who was still inside him was able to cry himself out, until—at last—he didn't need to cry anymore.

"What's wrong? Why are you crying?" she asked.

"You're a very pretty girl," was all that he could say.

"Thank you."

He lifted his hands away from her face. "That bus might be awhile," he said softly after a long moment of silence.

"You think so?"

"Yes. But don't worry, I'll wait here with you."

"That's nice of you."

"Don't mention it. It's my pleasure."

And together they waited.

The Ghost Hunters

"Is that the place?" Doug asked Stephanie, indicating the large broken-down estate at the end of the road. He tried to sound cool and nonchalant, but it was obvious that he was excited. This was his first "Documentation Mission" with Stephanie and her husband, Jordan, and he couldn't wait to get inside and look for ghosts.

"That's it," Stephanie nodded. "Wooster Mansion." She grabbed her notebook from her backpack and read aloud from it. "It was built around 1926 by a guy named Wilburforce Wooster—"

"Wilburforce?" Jordan interrupted.

Stephanie shrugged. "Don't look at me, I didn't name him. Parents can be cruel though, huh?" She let Doug and Jordan agree with her before she continued. "So, anyway, he built this place for his family after moving here from New York, which apparently they weren't too happy about."

"I don't blame them," Doug sympathized. "I wouldn't be too happy if I had to move from the big city to the most boring place on earth." Doug had lived in Tarryville for three years now. His family had moved there when he was 15 and he considered meeting Stephanie and Jordan the only remotely interesting thing to have happened to him in that time.

Strangely, given how small the town was, his first encounter with them wasn't in person, but on the Internet. Long fascinated by the world of the supernatural, he had spent an idle Sunday searching for websites about ghosts on his dad's computer. Purely by chance, one of the first sites he came across was the one run by Stephanie and Jordan. On it he found hundreds of photos taken in old and abandoned buildings, as well as better-maintained historical sites. No matter the locale, each photo had one thing in common: an orb, one of the floating balls of light that many believe are the wandering souls of the dead. Doug became excited when he realized that the people who had taken these pictures lived in the same town he did. Many of the pictures were taken in buildings he had walked past many times, and it thrilled him to learn that he had been right all along when he had suspected that they were haunted. As soon as he had finished exploring every page the site had to offer, he sent the couple an email message with his phone number in it and urged them to call him the next time they went to "document" a house. Two days later he found himself on the phone with Stephanie, a charming woman who turned out to be only six years older than he was. She invited him to come along with them for their trip through the Wooster Mansion, and he eagerly accepted.

A young couple just out of university, Stephanie and Jordan had come together when they discovered that they shared all the same obsessions. Both were dedicated to the scientific analysis of the supernatural and to British science-fiction TV shows of the 1970s, and, figuring that few people could ever be more compatible, they got married and settled in Jordan's hometown, where they commuted to the big city for their day jobs. Stephanie worked as a researcher for a marketing firm and Jordan managed one of New York's largest comic book stores. Despite the long hours they spent at work, they still managed to find time to devote to their website, their greatest passion. Every weekend they gathered up their equipment and found some new place to explore and then carefully documented what they found on their website. When they got Doug's email message, they were thrilled to find someone in Tarryville who understood their zeal, and they happily invited him to join them.

Stephanie continued to read from her notebook.

"In fact, his kids were so mad about moving to Tarryville they actually plotted to kill him."

"Really?" asked Doug, unaware that anything so macabre could actually happen in Tarryville. "How old were they?"

"In their 20s and 30s, I think."

Doug snorted. "Why didn't they just stay in New York then?"

"According to what I found on the Net, Wilburforce insisted that his family be with him wherever he went and he threatened to disinherit anyone who left him."

"What a freak!" laughed Jordan.

"Yeah," Stephanie agreed, "I'm surprised he lasted as long as he did. Everyone lived here for three years before they finally killed him."

"How'd they do it?" asked Doug.

"I'm not sure. I checked everywhere I could and it appears that no one ever found his body. They managed to get rid of it somehow, which is why no one was ever charged for the crime."

"Did they get his money?" asked Jordan.

"Actually, they didn't. Because they couldn't find his body they had to wait before they could declare him legally dead. During that time, all his investments began to fail and when they were finally able to start divvying everything up, there was nothing left to divvy. All that was left was the house, which they tried to sell, but no one would buy it."

"What happened to them?" asked Doug.

"I don't know," Stephanie admitted. "They just left, I guess. The place has sat empty for close to 70 years. It belongs to the city now, but they don't seem to have any plans for it. It's a pity when you think about it. This place would make a wonderful museum."

Doug pretended to ponder this before he grinned and clapped his hands together. "So are you guys ready?" he asked them, infecting them with his giddiness.

They smiled and nodded, grabbed their cameras and bags and followed him as he practically ran towards the old house. When he got to the front door, he stopped and waited impatiently for them to join him.

"C'mon!" he shouted. "They aren't getting any deader!"

Jordan and Stephanie both laughed. Doug's enthusiasm reminded them of the way they had acted when they had first started, and it made what was a standard trip for them into something special. They hurried their pace and joined him at the front door.

"How do we get in?" asked Doug.

"That depends," Jordan answered. "Have you tried opening the door?"

Doug looked at him doubtfully before he tried turning the doorknob. It was rusty and stubborn but wasn't locked, and the heavy door swung open.

"That was easy," said Doug. "Are abandoned houses usually left open for anyone to get in?"

"Almost never," Stephanie answered.

"But it doesn't hurt to try," Jordan added.

The two of them couldn't help smiling as they watched Doug walk through the doorway. His moves were careful and hesitant, as if the devil himself was hiding behind the door and ready to attack. They, on the other hand, were much more relaxed. By now they knew that their biggest danger was that they might step on a loose nail and require a tetanus shot.

As they walked from the foyer into the mansion's living room, the first thing they saw was the dust floating in the sunlight that shone through its large bay window. Jordan and Stephanie both took a picture of it.

"Do orbs gravitate towards sunlight?" asked Doug.

"Not really," Stephanie shrugged, "but it is pretty."

Thanks to the sunlight they saw that the room not only was still furnished, but was full of the type of antiques that people appeared on television to brag about finding.

"That's weird," remarked Jordan.

"What?" asked Doug.

"Places like this are almost always empty, and when they're not, all you find are things people couldn't be bothered to take with them."

Stephanie agreed. "This stuff is way too nice to just leave behind."

"Maybe they couldn't decide who'd get everything and decided just to leave it," Doug suggested.

"Maybe," admitted Jordan, "but that still wouldn't explain why it's still here. I mean, how strange is it for a place that's sat unprotected for 70 years to go undisturbed? Thieves should have cleaned this place out decades ago."

"I guess people in Tarryville are above that sort of thing," said Doug.

Both Jordan and Stephanie stared at him as if he was an idiot.

"I'm joking!" he insisted. "It's probably just that no one knew this stuff was still here."

They both nodded noncommittally and started to take pictures.

"I don't see anything," complained Doug. "Where are the orbs?"

Jordan smiled. "They only appear on film," he explained. "I thought you knew that."

"Yeah, I do," Doug admitted, "but still, I expected to see *something*."

His older companions laughed at this and continued to take pictures around the room. Doug quickly grew bored and sat down on a very dusty but still exquisite sofa. As he did, he heard a quiet moan. He looked over to Jordan and Stephanie and saw that it wasn't coming from them. Self-consciously he looked down at his own stomach, knowing he had skipped breakfast that morning, but it too was quiet. The sound was muffled and muted, but as he listened to it he could hear that it sounded like someone trying to speak.

"*Geeeeeeeeeettttttttt ouuuuuuuuuutttttttttt.*"

All the blood drained from Doug's face as he slowly turned his head and tried to find the source of the message. With a look of terrified confusion he realized that it was coming from directly under him. He jumped up like a shot and the moan continued, clearer than before.

"*Geeeeeeeeeettttttttt ouuuuuuuuuutttttttttt.*"

"What'd you say?" asked Jordan as he took another picture.

Doug pointed at the spot on the sofa where he had just been sitting and tried to speak, but all he could manage was panicked gibberish.

"What's going on?" asked Stephanie.

Doug started to back away from the sofa, while still pointing to the source of the sound.

"*Geeeeeeeeeettttttttt ouuuuuuuuuutttttttttt.*"

"What is that?" Stephanie and Jordan asked at the same time.

"Ghost," Doug managed under his breath, "in the sofa."

Stephanie rolled her eyes. "Very funny, Doug. What'd you do? Hide a tape recorder down there?"

He shook his head slowly, but that wasn't enough to stop her from walking over to the sofa and flipping up the cushion.

A flash of nauseating green light instantly overtook the room; it stank of decades worth of rot and decay. With it, the voice spoke once again, but now—freed from the muffling effects of the sofa's cushion—it was much louder and easier to understand.

"*GET OUT!*" it bellowed at them with heart-stopping fury before the light vanished as quickly as it had appeared.

All three of them screamed and immediately ran for the door. Before they could reach it, it swung itself shut with a heavy slam and a definite click. Jordan got to it first and tried to open it, but it was locked tight. He tried knocking it down by running up against it, but all that did was almost dislocate his shoulder. They then tried to escape by breaking one of the windows, but everything they threw disintegrated like a misty haze in the air before it could reach the glass.

"You can't do that!" Doug ranted. "You can't tell people to get out and then make it impossible for them to leave!"

The three of them cowered in the foyer as they tried to catch their breath. Outside the sun was overtaken by a large mass of black storm clouds and the house grew ominously dark.

"Okay," Doug huffed and puffed, "what do we do now?"

"How should we know?" answered a still shaking Stephanie.

"You guys are experts at this," Doug reminded her. "You've done this hundreds of times before."

"We've never done this before," Jordan disagreed.

"Yes, you have. You have the pictures on your website," Doug insisted.

Jordan and Stephanie both shook their heads.

"We take pictures of floating spheres of light," answered Stephanie, "and that"—she pointed towards the now quiet living room—"is something we have never seen before."

"That's like a..." Jordan struggled to find the right words "...real ghost or something."

Now more disillusioned than afraid, Doug rolled his eyes. "Some ghost hunters you guys turned out to be."

With that he stood up and headed back into the living room.

"What are you doing?" asked Stephanie.

"We've got to get out of here somehow," he told them, "and we're not going to do it by shivering in a corner. So you guys can both get up and follow me or stay there forever. It's up to you." He then turned back around and headed out of the doorway at the other side of the living room into the unexplored part of the house.

Jordan and Stephanie looked at each other before they jumped up and ran after their younger colleague. They found him in a darkened hallway, searching in his backpack for his flashlight. They got theirs out too and together the three lights managed to break through the windowless gloom. Along the hallway's walls they saw a series of portraits, some of which were paintings and others photographs. As they studied each of them it quickly became clear that the Woosters were not known for their good looks.

"Wow, are these guys ugly or what?" marveled Doug as he looked at a photo of Wilburforce's youngest daughter, Eunice.

"Shhhhh," Jordan scolded him, "one of them might be the ghost and he might not appreciate you calling him ugly!"

Doug nodded silently at this before he started to move towards the stairs. Jordan and Stephanie hesitantly followed him as he walked up its steps.

"Do you hear that?" asked Stephanie when they were halfway up the staircase.

"No. What is it?" asked Jordan.

"I don't know. It's like a dripping sound."

"I don't hear anything," Doug insisted as he reached the top of the stairs, but he quickly changed his mind when he turned to the right. The beam of his flashlight caught the sight of Eunice's unattractive face as it hovered 3 feet off the ground. Blood dripped from her neck onto the floor and she hissed at him the now-familiar phrase *"GET OUT!"*

Doug screamed a scream so shrill a five-year-old girl would have had difficulty topping it. He turned around and nearly collided with Jordan and Stephanie as he ran past them down the stairs. In his haste he dropped his flashlight and failed, as he reached the main floor, to see the wall in front of him. He slammed into it with a frightening crunch, and the photo of Eunice he had just maligned crashed painfully onto his head.

"Are you okay?" asked Stephanie as she and Jordan raced back down the stairs.

"I'm fine," Doug insisted, but the way those two words slurred together suggested otherwise. "Just give me a sec."

Jordan and Stephanie waited impatiently as Doug tried to stand up. They tried to help him, but he protested that he was okay and didn't need to be babied. Finally, he managed to get to his feet and started to walk towards the two of them. He didn't make it two steps before his legs gave out from under him. Luckily, Jordan managed to catch him before he crashed to the ground.

Jordan and Stephanie placed the now-delirious Doug in an empty space underneath the stairs while they tried to decide what to do next.

"What are our options?" Jordan asked his wife.

"Well, we've got to find a way to get out of here, which means either we leave him here by himself or one of us stays with him while the other searches around."

"I don't think we can leave him by himself," answered Jordan.

"Okay, then one of us will stay with him," Stephanie nodded. "Who's going to search for a way out of here?" The tone of her voice indicated that she expected her big strong husband to volunteer. He didn't.

"Flip you for it," he offered, digging in his right pocket for a coin.

"Fine," she rolled her eyes, silently calculating how much she could get in the divorce settlement if he actually made her do it.

"Heads!" Stephanie shouted as he threw the quarter into the air. Jordan caught it and placed it on the back of his hand. It was tails.

"So," she glared at him, "I guess you'll stay with him while I—your dainty and defenseless young bride—will walk around this haunted mansion and try to find a way for us to get out of here."

"Uh-huh," Jordan agreed.

"You sure you can handle it?"

If Jordan heard the withering sarcasm in his wife's question, he chose to ignore it.

"I think so," he answered, leaving her no clue as to whether or not he was deliberately being obtuse.

With daggers in her eyes, Stephanie turned away from her husband and went back up the staircase. Furious at him, she forgot all about how scared she was and stormed up the staircase as quickly as she could. When she got to the top, she found that whatever had scared Doug so badly was no longer there. Pointing her flashlight towards the dark upstairs hallway, she saw only a collection of six closed doors, three on the left and three on the right.

Almost as soon as it disappeared, her fear returned when she realized she was going to have to explore what was in those rooms. Slowly and cautiously she walked towards the first door on the right and grasped the knob, half-hoping that the door was locked. It wasn't. The door creaked cinematically as she pushed it open and exposed a large, ornately decorated room that had obviously been Wilburforce's bedroom.

A huge canopy bed dominated its center and would have been the focus of attention if it were not for the huge marble fireplace that took up almost the entire left wall. Above its mantle was another portrait of Wilburforce, but this one showed an older man than the one she had seen downstairs. Remembering her reason for being there, she walked over to the room's window and tried to open it. It wouldn't budge, and when she threw a heavy ashtray at it, it vanished right before it hit the glass. It then occurred to her that they might be able to climb up the fireplace's chimney. She walked over to it, crouched down and crawled into the huge hearth, which was full of dark heavy ash that got all over her clothes. She looked up the flue, but all she saw was darkness, and as she searched the blackness for any sign that her plan might be feasible, she heard the sound of a door slamming shut.

Her face blackened by ash, she popped her head out of the fireplace and saw that the room's door was now closed. She got up and ran to it and found that it was locked. Terrified, she began to scream and pound on it with her fists.

"Be quiet!" a voice shouted at her from inside the room.

Stephanie's heart skipped a beat, and she slowly turned towards the room. It was still empty. She pointed her flashlight at everything she could in a frantic search to locate the source of the voice, but she found nothing.

"I am up here," the voice said, sighing impatiently.

Stephanie followed the sound and looked up. She saw that the words were coming from the portrait of Wilburforce Wooster. Amazed, she walked over to it and shone her flashlight on it.

"Do you mind?" Wilburforce sniffed. "The light is shining in my eyes."

"Oh, sorry," Stephanie replied.

She could see that the portrait of the man had come alive. It was still made of oil paint, but it moved as if it were animated.

"Why are you here?" Wilburforce demanded.

"We just came to take some pictures and explore a bit," Stephanie explained as she tried to stop shaking.

"Why? To steal from me?"

"No, just to see if we could find some ghosts."

"Well, if that is the case, why do you look so frightened? You have found what you were searching for after all."

"You weren't the kind of ghosts we were looking for."

"What other kind are there?"

"Orbs," she mumbled weakly.

"Excuse me?"

"Floating balls of light that appear only on film," she explained.

Wilburforce pondered this for a moment before he exploded in a burst of laughter. Oil paint tears began to fall down his cheeks as he doubled over, holding onto his stomach.

"That is the most ridiculous thing I've ever heard," he finally managed after he was able to stop a loud coughing fit brought on by his merriment.

Stephanie frowned and crossed her arms.

"I am sorry," he said. "I did not mean to offend you. I suppose everyone needs a hobby."

"Look, make fun of us if you want," Stephanie replied. "Just explain to me why all you ghosts keep screaming at us to get out, but you won't let us leave."

"Ah," Wilburforce smiled, "the mistake you have made is assuming that we are all of the same mindset. The ghosts you have encountered who are so intent on seeing you go are the spirits of my children, who want you to leave before you discover the truth about this house. I, on the other hand, am responsible for keeping you here. I cannot let you leave until the truth is exposed."

"What truth?"

"I was murdered, but my body was never found. Find out what happened to it and who was responsible and I will let you go."

"Promise?"

"I swear, but you should know that my children will do all that they can to stop you from finding out."

"Yeah, I figured that out already."

Wilburforce's portrait smiled at this and froze back into place. The room's door creaked open and Stephanie ran downstairs to tell Jordan and Doug what she had just been told. When she got to where she had left them, underneath the stairs, she found that they were gone.

Stephanie swore loudly and began to shout out their names. There was no response, save for a sickening silence punctuated by the thunder that had begun to rumble outside.

"You can't do this to me!" she shouted at the house, the ghosts and, in particular, her two cohorts.

She ran back up the stairs and tried to go back into Wilburforce's bedroom, but she stopped when she saw who was standing in front of his door. It was the skeletal remains of his oldest son, Winthrop. He was identifiable by the three rings he wore on his bony index finger. They were the same rings she had noticed in his portrait earlier.

Apparently Winthrop lacked the ability to speak because all he could manage was a deep and threatening hiss, but despite this his message was clear. Slowly he moved towards Stephanie, who had become frozen with terror. Like a deer in the headlights, all she could do was stare helplessly as the walking corpse moved towards her. She tried to scream, but she couldn't make a sound. Winthrop edged closer and closer towards her. He was just a foot away when she closed her eyes and prayed that it would be over quickly. She held her breath and waited and listened as he approached. She felt the stench that came from his mouth hit her nose as he moved just inches from her body. Finally she managed to scream. As she wailed she heard a loud thud, followed by a louder one. She opened her eyes and saw her husband in front of her holding a large candlestick. At her feet were Winthrop's body and the dusty remnants of his skull.

"What?" Jordan said as she stared at him. "You didn't think we'd let you do this alone, did you?"

All at once Stephanie managed to scream, laugh and cry, while she hugged and punched her husband repeatedly.

"Don't you ever do that to me again!" she ordered him tearfully with a grateful smile. "Where's Doug?"

"Right here!" she heard him pipe up from behind Jordan.

"How are you doing?"

"Fine. I don't think I'm supposed to see these flashing lights all the time, but beyond that I'm much better now."

"Where did you guys go?" she asked them.

"We followed you up here and starting exploring the other rooms," Jordan explained, "but we couldn't find a way to get out."

"You're not going to," Stephanie informed him, and then she told them what she had learned from the painting of Wilburforce Wooster.

"Okay, let me get this straight," Doug said slowly after she finished. "The painting moved? Like it was alive?"

Stephanie nodded.

"That's it," swore Doug. "I am *never* going into another haunted house ever, *ever*, again."

Jordan placed a comforting hand on Doug's shoulder. "How about we worry about getting out of here before we say things like that?"

"But how are we supposed to do that?" asked Doug. "You heard what she said. We can't get out of here until we discover the truth."

Jordan shrugged. "Then we discover the truth. It's gotta be around here somewhere, and I don't know about you but I've read plenty of mysteries. I can't see this one being too difficult to figure out. Let's just think about it. What do we already know?"

"We know Wilburforce was killed," answered Stephanie.

"Right, and who did it?"

"His kids," Doug joined in.

"Right. So all we have to figure out is how they did it and where they got rid of the body. Easy. It's not as if there are a lot of options for that sort of thing."

From outside a flash of lightning and its corresponding crack of thunder interrupted the silence in which they tried to think of different ways to kill a person and permanently dispose of a body.

"Now think about it," Jordan continued. "These guys were rich, and what's the last thing rich people want to deal with?" He didn't give them time enough to answer him. "A mess. The last thing they would want to do is clean up a lot of blood and guts and all the other stuff that comes with shooting, stabbing or clubbing someone to death. They would want something that was clean and easy."

"Poison!" Stephanie caught up with him.

"Exactly!"

"So what do we do? Find the poison?" asked Doug doubtfully.

"You've got a better idea?"

"Okay," Doug shrugged. "Do you want to split up or search together?"

"Together," Stephanie and Jordan answered in unison.

Over the next hour the three of them searched the house for anything that could be considered poisonous.

They started in the kitchen, hoping to find some rat poison or some sort of dangerous cleaning product, but all they found were some old pots and pans and some ancient tins that would go for a small fortune if they were sold in an auction. They tried the basement next, where they were met by the floating white apparition of Wilburforce's middle daughter, Mildred. She screamed at them something fierce, but by now the trio's fear had turned to annoyance and they ignored the shouting spirit and searched the musty cellar for anything toxic. Again they came up empty and decided to go back upstairs and search the rooms of the five children.

They started in Eunice's room. It was a frilly, feminine room with yellowing lace attached to almost everything in it. Dolls sat throughout the room on shelves and furniture and stared at them while they searched.

Doug whispered to Stephanie while they both looked under the bed.

"I think they"—he nodded towards a group of curly-haired dolls to their right—"scare me more than the ghosts do."

Stephanie nodded silently in agreement.

"I've found something!" Jordan shouted from the closet he had been searching.

"What?" asked Doug as he and Stephanie both got up.

"I don't know, but it's in a small brown bottle. The label's so faded I can't make out what it is."

"So it could be poison, or it could be cough syrup," Stephanie frowned.

"How many people hide bottles of cough syrup in boxes inside their closet?" Jordan countered.

"My cousin Stephen," Doug answered, "but we're not supposed to talk about it."

"Let's just take it with us," Stephanie suggested, "and search the other rooms in case we can find something more concrete."

Both Doug and Jordan agreed that this was a good idea, and they moved on to Winthrop's room. His room was much more sparsely decorated than his sister's and reflected someone with a somber and serious philosophy. The room was so spartan that it didn't take them long to declare it empty of anything harmful to humans. They were about to leave when Stephanie took note of an empty pot on Winthrop's dresser. She walked over to it and grabbed it. It was full of dry and crusty dirt.

"What about this?" she asked the others.

"There's nothing in it," Jordan shrugged.

"Now, yeah, but what if this had at some point contained some deadly plant or herb or root or something? It would have died by now, but think about it, how many guys as boring as this would bother to keep a plant in their room?"

"Well, my cousin Stephen—" Doug began before he was silenced by a dirty look from Stephanie.

Jordan nodded. "Let's take it with us and keep looking."

In a dresser drawer in Mildred's room they found a small metal box filled with little white pills. They debated whether they could be a potentially fatal narcotic or really old mints. They decided to bring them along and continue the search.

The powerful odor in the next room they entered made it clear that it had belonged to the first ghost they encountered. According to the diary Jordan found, his name was Brewster.

"Brewster Wooster?" marveled Doug. "Sometimes I think this Wilburforce guy deserved to be killed. Wait a minute, I think I found something."

From under Brewster's bed, Doug lifted out a small box whose lid bore a name too faded to make out. He opened it and found a fine white powder.

"Okay," he said, picking some up and grinding it between his fingers, "this is either some kind of deadly poison or a foot fungus remedy."

In the last room, which by default had to belong to Wilburforce's youngest son, Desmond, they found nothing that even remotely resembled a deadly toxin, but something else caught Stephanie's eye as she rummaged through the clothes that hung in his closet.

"Take a look at this," she said as she pulled out a suit that was covered in ash.

"These people were rich, didn't they know about dry cleaning?" asked Doug.

"The only way these people's clothes got clean was if the servants washed them for them, and if they ran out of money after their dad died, they'd have had no one to do it for them," Stephanie explained.

"You don't think—?" Jordan had the same idea as his wife.

"Yeah, he was wearing this when he got rid of the body, and I know exactly where he did it."

The three walked into Wilburforce's bedroom.

"Is that the painting?" asked Doug with an uneasy expression on his face.

Stephanie nodded before she cleared her throat and approached the portrait.

"Mr. Wooster? Are you there?"

The sound of thunder cracked loudly as they waited for an answer. Behind them the room's door swung shut with a heavy slam and the old man in the painting yawned.

"Back so soon?" he spoke to Stephanie.

"Yes, sir," she answered respectfully. "I think we found some evidence that might lead us to the truth."

"Go on."

"It occurred to us that your children might have been a little squeamish when it came to violence—"

"They were a bunch of spoiled brats who didn't like to get their hands dirty is what you mean," Wilburforce interrupted her.

"Yes, sir," Stephanie continued. "So we assumed that they must have poisoned you."

"That does sound like them, gutless cowards that they were."

"So we searched their rooms and we found these."

Doug and Jordan held up the flowerpot, the brown bottle and the cardboard and metal boxes.

"We can't prove what any of them are, but they are all suspicious. And we found this." She held up Desmond's old suit. "We think he was wearing this when he put you into this fireplace and cremated your remains."

"You *think?* That's not good enough!" the painting bellowed at them. "I need to know!"

"But all these could be poisons," Doug protested. "Any one of them could have done it. There's no way for us to know."

"I have to know!" Wilburforce's portrait grew red in the face.

Silence took over the room as the three of them stared helplessly at the enraged painting. Doug had never felt so hopeless in all his life, as he imagined himself being forced to spend the rest of his days trapped in the horrible house. He turned his head to look outside the room's window and despaired that he would never get to see the world outside again. Then, simultaneously, thunder roared and lightning struck a tree just outside the window.

"I got it!" he shouted.

"What?" Stephanie, Jordan and the painting all asked at once.

"They all hated you," he said to the painting, "right?"

"Yes."

"And all these could be poisons, right?"

"So you say."

"Then what if they're *all* poisons. What if they all tried to kill you?"

Jordan looked doubtful. "At the same time? What are the chances of that?"

"Dude," Doug rolled his eyes, "you're standing in front of a moving painting. All of them coincidentally poisoning him on the same day isn't that huge of a stretch."

Wilburforce's portrait thought about this.

"Those buffoons all did think alike. It isn't inconceivable that they would all try to kill me at the same time. In fact, it would shock me if it were otherwise."

Doug, Jordan and Stephanie all held their breaths and waited as the old man in their painting mulled over everything he had learned.

"I am satisfied," he finally decided, allowing them to exhale with relief. "You may go."

"Thank God," Doug sighed. "I was afraid if we stayed here any longer Desmond would come out of somewhere and do what his siblings couldn't."

Jordan and Stephanie stared at Doug in disbelief.

"I probably shouldn't have said that," Doug admitted.

In front of them a howling wind formed inside the fireplace. The ashes inside it swirled and joined together and took the shape of a young, angry-looking man. He stepped out of the fireplace and roared at the three ghost hunters. Before he could do anything else, Jordan, Stephanie and Doug ran as though wings were attached to their feet. Desmond's ghost flew after them, but his anger was no match for their terror, and they made it out of the house before he even got down the stairs.

The three of them ran to their car, jumped into it and drove away as fast as the floored pedal would take them. When, at last, they felt they had traveled a safe distance, they slowed down and rode silently back towards their homes. No one said a word during the drive. Jordan and Stephanie dropped Doug off at his house, where in the rain he dropped down on his knees and kissed the sidewalk. They drove away and he went inside and threw away all his books about the supernatural. Now that he had seen the real thing, they weren't that interesting.

Jordan and Stephanie had the same reaction. As they drove home they agreed that was the last time they would ever go into a haunted house. When they got home they went to their computer and left a message explaining to their loyal online followers that their website would be closing and that they were going to pursue a new endeavor, which would probably have something to do with the '70s British science fiction that they loved. As they began to dismantle their site they took one last look at all the photographs they had taken over the years.

"Do you think they're really ghosts?" Jordan asked his wife as they sat together and pondered a photograph they had taken on their very first mission. In it two large and vibrant orbs floated above the mantelpiece of a grand decaying fireplace. They had always considered it their best picture and had used it on their website as the one piece of photographic evidence skeptics would find hardest to dispute.

Stephanie took some time before she answered him. She thought about what the cranky old ghost in the oil painting had said to her after he had wiped away his tears of laughter.

"Does it matter?" she finally answered Jordan. "Everyone needs a hobby, and"—she smiled as she deleted the file from their hard drive—"they sure were pretty."

The Chronicler

With a tired yawn, Donald ambled over to the office's printer and grabbed the 10 pages or so that he had just extracted from the Internet. He browsed through them as he walked back to his small cubicle. Then he sat down, took a long sip of coffee and reread the passage he was interested in.

THE MYSTERY OF OLD BOGIE

In 1873, an old prospector named Zephaniah Bogart bought a small stake of land near the small town of God's Promise, Nevada. Very little is known about him except that he was a quiet man who preferred to be left alone. He had bought the land with the last of his savings with the hopes that it would provide him with enough gold that he would be able to retire within the next three years. He never expected that he would end up uncovering a vein of gold so large and pure it would have made him one of the wealthiest men in America, if he had lived.

Unfortunately for him, the same day he came across this life-changing discovery, a gang of robbers who had just robbed the bank in God's Promise descended upon his camp. There they found the old prospector carrying some nuggets he had taken as samples from his exciting new find. The robbers demanded that he give them the gold and tell them where he had gotten it. He gave them the samples willingly, but he refused to show the criminals where he had found them. They shot him dead and spent the next three days searching for the gold but couldn't find it. They were still looking when the sheriff came and arrested them for robbing the bank and for killing Bogart. The four men all went to prison where they told everyone they met about the small stretch of land near God's Promise, Nevada, that was home to a well-hidden vein of pure gold.

Many of the men who heard the story remembered it when they were released from prison and went out in search for the unclaimed treasure. One of them was a gambler named Henderson, who found the land he had heard described by one of the original robbers as soon as he was released. It was a cold and rainy night and Henderson was ill prepared for the outdoors. He had never camped out before and wouldn't have stayed if it were not for his desire to get his hands on Bogart's hidden gold. Even though it was pitch black out and the rain was coming down so hard he almost had to swim through it, he decided to start looking right then and there. All he managed to do was get muddy, but his actions were still enough to raise the ire of the spirit of Zephaniah Bogart.

Ever since Bogart had died refusing to disclose the location of his gold, his ghost had remained on the land in order to protect it from being found. Every man who came to find the hidden treasure didn't stay for long after being confronted by the angry phantom. Of them all, Henderson was the one who was most affected by the encounter.

Henderson flailed about in the rain, without a clue about how to find the gold or what to do if he did find it. While he searched he looked up and saw a man floating in front of him. It was so dark out that he normally wouldn't have been able to see anything, but the man in front of him glowed with a bright white light. "Git off my land!" the old spirit ordered the terrified gambler. Henderson turned around as fast as he could and started to run. His feet slipped in the mud and he fell hard against a large jagged rock. He screamed in pain as his leg snapped in two. Bogart's ghost disappeared and Henderson lay there for two days before a local hunter found him. By the time a doctor could treat him, his leg had become so infected that there was no choice but to amputate it. Whenever someone asked Henderson how he lost his leg, he would always tell them the story of the phantom prospector.

Even now there are people who insist that the ghost of Zephaniah Bogart still haunts the land where he was killed. Though sightings of the spirit have become rarer and rarer throughout the years, many claim to have spotted him while searching for his gold, which—to this day—has never been found.

Donald yawned again and took another long sip from his coffee as he tried to think of any details he could add to make this story more interesting.

Donald's job was to write (or rather rewrite) ghost stories. For the first part of the day he would look for true accounts of ghosts from various sources, and when he found one he thought he could work with, he would spend the rest of the day turning it into something he could use for his latest book. Donald didn't believe in ghosts and had never had anything close to a paranormal experience but still got the job of researching and writing done.

After he read the story about the dead prospector one more time, Donald concluded that it lacked sex appeal and wasn't scary enough, plus he hated its lack of a real ending. He decided to try to recreate the basic story and take some liberties with the facts he'd found—add some interesting details and imagined motivation to the characters. He thought about this and a few minutes later he started typing. By the end of the day he had finished the story.

DEAD MAN'S GOLD

Zephaniah Bogart was a gambling man. A prospector by trade, he seldom was able to hold onto the money he earned for longer than a day or two. But one lucky night he was dealt all the right cards and for the first time in his life, he walked away a winner with more money than he could earn in 10 years. While he counted his earnings, a grizzled heap of a man named Kendrick, who had witnessed Bogart's good fortune, approached him with a deal.

"I've got me a nice piece of land," the old man told Bogart, "but I'm too old to do anything with it. It's yours for $50, if you want it."

Bogart hesitated. He wasn't sure about this deal.

"I've also got myself a daughter," Kendrick continued, "and she's a peach if I say so myself. Buy the land and I'll let you marry her."

This got Bogart interested. Everyone around the town of God's Promise, Nevada, knew about Kendrick's daughter, Charlotte. She was a tall, brazen, blonde beauty with the type of figure most men would willingly sacrifice a year's pay to touch. Bogart spent months and months by himself prospecting, and the idea of being able to bring a beautiful woman with him to keep him company was appealing.

"You got a deal!" he said, shaking hands with Kendrick.

The very next night the justice of the peace presided over the marriage of Bogart and Charlotte. Beneath his furry tuft of beard, the prospector was pink with joy, but his bride wasn't nearly as pleased.

Understandably, Charlotte wasn't thrilled about the idea of basically being sold to the scraggly older man. But back in those days, a woman had very few rights and was essentially considered the property of her father or husband, so there was little that she could do.

The next day, the two newlyweds spent their honeymoon traveling to the land Bogart had bought from Charlotte's father. With the rest of his gambling fortune, Bogart had purchased a horse, a buggy and enough supplies to last them six months. It took them a day and a half to get there, and what they found proved to be not quite what Kendrick had promised. The land was muddy and full of hard stones and small dying trees.

Charlotte sneered when she saw it. "Only a fool would spend money to own a place like this," she snorted disdainfully.

Those were the nicest words she ever said to him.

Over the next few months, as Bogart tried to recoup his investment by finding some kind of precious metal on the property, Charlotte became nastier and nastier. A vicious shrew, she hounded his every move and laughed at his every mistake. It soon became clear that this was the worst deal Bogart had ever made.

But then something happened that proved that even in a person's darkest hours there is always the possibility of seeing the light. Tired of listening to Charlotte nag him about building them a real place to live rather than the tent they stayed in now, he started digging in the muddy ground to find the sturdiest spot to erect a cabin. It was while he was digging that his shovel hit something hard in the ground. Intrigued, he quickly dug around it and was excited to discover that he had unearthed a large wooden chest. He tried to lift it out of the hole, but it was so heavy he couldn't get it out. While it still lay in the ground, he used his shovel to break off the old lock that kept the chest shut and he opened it up. For a moment he felt as if he might faint. His hand began to shake when he picked up the largest nugget of gold he had ever seen. It was the size of an apple, and a quick inspection of the chest's other contents proved that it was, in fact, the smallest chunk of gold the chest contained.

As quickly as he could, he reburied the chest, leaving out only the apple-sized chunk so he could show it to Charlotte. Before he left his treasure to find her he lifted up the gigantic nugget and admired it as it gleamed in the sun.

"I'll bet she'll stop pestering me now," he smiled.

What Bogart did not know was that at the exact moment he discovered his treasure, his beautiful young wife was making a discovery of her own. She had been walking through the muddy land, bored out of her mind trying to find something to do, when she heard what sounded like a man breathing. Never a timid woman, she approached the sound and was shocked and delighted to find that it was coming from a handsome young man. Not only that, he was also a handsome young man Charlotte had known very well in town. His name was Rusty and he was just the type of raffish cad a woman like Charlotte went for.

"What happened to you?" she asked him when she saw that he was injured.

"The sheriff thought I tried to rob the bank and he shot at me as I rode away," answered Rusty, "but this wound is only skin deep. I hurt myself much more when I fell off my horse."

"You poor thing," she cooed, hugging him sympathetically. "Why did the sheriff think you tried to rob the bank?"

Rusty smiled guiltily. " 'Cause I tried to rob it," he admitted.

Charlotte laughed at this. "You're just so naughty, aren't you?"

Before Rusty could answer her, the two of them heard the sound of Charlotte's name being shouted in the distance. Charlotte frowned.

"That's my husband," she sighed wearily.

"I heard about that. Fat Jack told me your father sold you and this land to old Zephaniah Bogart for $50. Struck me as a darn shame. You're worth at least twice that in my books."

Charlotte blushed. "You sweet-talker," she giggled.

Bogart's shouts became louder and louder.

"I better go and see what he wants," Charlotte groaned.

"Don't tell him I'm here," Rusty told her.

"Don't worry, I won't."

Charlotte then got up and ran towards her husband's voice. When she found him he was shaking and out of breath and something shined mightily in his hand.

"What is that?" she asked him.

He held it up to her. "That is the largest piece of gold you've ever seen," he told her, "and it's the smallest one I found."

"Where are the rest?"

"In a safe spot for now."

Charlotte screamed and started jumping up and down.

"I thought this would make you happy," Bogart laughed, but before he could gloat she turned away from him and started running towards Rusty.

She was breathless when she got to him and it took her a moment to explain to him why she was so excited, but she managed to get the words out. Suddenly all of Rusty's pain vanished from his body and he jumped up and hugged Charlotte. Together the two of them ran towards Bogart.

"Who is this?" Bogart asked when he saw Rusty.

Rusty answered by punching the prospector in the jaw. Bogart fell to the ground and the younger man jumped on top of him.

"Tell us where the gold is, old man!" he ordered threateningly.

Bogart stayed quiet. Rusty grabbed the nugget that was still in the older man's hand and lifted it up. It was heavy enough to be used as a lethal weapon. He held it over his head and ordered Bogart one last time to tell him where the rest of the gold was. Bogart still refused and Rusty smashed the large nugget into his head. He hit him four more times and then Bogart's body grew limp and lifeless underneath him.

"What did you do that for?" Charlotte whined. "Now how are we going to find the gold?"

"Don't you worry," Rusty smiled, "it's somewhere around here. We just have to find it."

Over the course of that night and the following day, the two of them dug holes all over the property, but they failed to find the buried gold. Charlotte was in the middle of digging another hole when a painful stench hit her nose. It was then that she remembered that she and Rusty had left Bogart's dead body on the ground where he had been murdered. She looked around to find Rusty and shouted over to him when she saw him.

"I think we better bury the old guy," she said. "He's getting a bit ripe."

Rusty hated the idea of wasting time on something that wasn't gold related, but his nose told him that Charlotte was right. Together the two of them dug a grave for the murdered prospector and dumped him in with a callous thud. They filled the hole as quickly as they could and went back to searching for the treasure.

Three days later they still had not found it and were beginning to get on each other's nerves.

"You damn fool!" Charlotte cursed at Rusty. "We'd be millionaires by now, if you hadn't killed him so quick."

"You keep your mouth shut," threatened Rusty. "I can find this gold all by myself, so you better act more civil if you know what's good for you!"

On the fourth day, it began to rain. Hundreds of holes dotted the landscape, but the gold had still not been found. Exhausted, Charlotte threw down her shovel and sat on the cold wet ground. Her entire body was covered with mud and her hands were raw and bloody from the almost nonstop digging. It was hard to look at her now and imagine that she was once the most desired woman in God's Promise. Rusty turned from his latest hole and caught her resting. He sneered and shouted over to her.

"We're never going to find it if all we do is sit around like a bunch of lazy jackasses!"

Charlotte glared at him, but she still stood back up and started digging another hole. Her anger energized her and she started working faster than she had before. As she tore up the ground at a feverish pace, she almost sprained her wrist when she suddenly hit a solid object. Her heart almost stopped when she realized that she had found the chest of gold. She was about to shout over to Rusty, when it occurred to her that she too did not need a partner and that she had little interest in sharing the treasure. With a smile on her face she stood up straight and walked over to Rusty. He looked up at her disdainfully and stopped digging.

"What do you want?" he asked impatiently.

With the smile still on her face, Charlotte lifted the shovel and swung it at Rusty's head. Caught completely unawares, Rusty didn't have time to react and he grunted painfully when the shovel slammed against his right ear. Stunned, he fell to the ground, where Charlotte hit him again and again, until she was sure he was dead. Then she walked back over to where she had found the chest and opened it up. Tears came to her eyes as she took in the beauty of the enormous chunks of gold. Time stood still as she stared at the gold. She became so enthralled that she no longer felt the rain falling or heard the slow methodical footsteps that were coming her way.

Her reverie was broken only when she felt a cold clammy hand touch her shoulder. She turned and screamed when she saw the rotting sunken face of her late husband. He was covered head to toe with mud, but that did not disguise the decay that had ravaged his body as he lay uncomfortably in his grave.

"How can this be?" Charlotte shrieked. "You're dead!"

"Had to come back," Bogart moaned, his words sounding lifeless and barren. "Need to take something with me..."

Terrified, Charlotte realized that she would have to sacrifice her treasure in order to save her life. "Take it!" she told the walking corpse. "Take it! It's all yours!"

The dead prospector slowly shook his decomposing head.

"Didn't come back for the gold," he said to her in his disturbing monotone. "Came back for you."

Charlotte screamed and tried to run, but the creature grabbed her by the arm and pulled her in close to him. She struggled and fought against him. She even tried to bite him, but his flesh just gave way in her mouth and he didn't even react. Slowly, he carried her back to the grave she and Rusty had dug for him, which was now open again thanks to the effort it took him to escape. He threw her into it, then jumped down with her and started to pull in the muddy ground around them. Charlotte's screams echoed throughout the land, until finally they were silenced under the ground.

A few days later the sheriff of God's Promise showed up at Bogart's stretch of land. He was looking for Rusty and soon found the bank robber lying dead on the muddy ground. He couldn't find Bogart and his wife, but he did find a large chest that was filled with what turned out to be iron sulfide, or—as it is more commonly known—fool's gold.

* * *

Donald didn't think it was his best effort, but he thought it was definitely a more exciting story than the original. With another yawn, he checked his watch and saw that it was time to go home, so he saved his story, got up and said good-bye to his coworkers.

He lived just a few blocks away from the office in a small one-bedroom apartment. He wasn't married or even dating at the moment, and he spent most nights watching television, playing video games or working on his own fiction, which had nothing at all to do with ghosts.

The first thing he did when he got home was turn his TV set on. A family sitcom appeared, and Donald let it play as he went into his kitchen to make dinner. Donald liked to cook, and he found that usually when he got started he lost all track of time and of what was going on around him. He was used to having the background noise from the TV, though, so he always kept it on. Today he decided to make his specialty, pan-fried chicken breasts with a green chili mustard sauce. As the television chirruped behind him, he gathered his ingredients and began cooking. It didn't take long for his attention to be completely taken over by his culinary efforts, so all he heard from his TV were out-of-context snatches of dialogue. He paid so little attention to them that he didn't notice how odd they sounded.

"But Mom," a young girl whined, "if Donald's a liar he must pay!"

"I know, dear," her mother answered. "He will."

"Are you sick and tired of being misrepresented?" an older-sounding man asked in a commercial. "If so, then call us at 1-800-GET-DONALD."

"*Waking up in the morning is tough / it can be really rough,*" a young woman sang in a coffee jingle, "*and it's time to tell the writer that enough is enough.*"

Forty minutes later, Donald's food was on his plate. He poured himself a glass of wine and sat down in front of his TV to eat. He flipped the channels as he ate and decided to stop on a music channel that was playing a video he really liked. As he watched it he realized that it must be a new version, because it was different from how he remembered it. In the original version, the lead singer and the actress playing his girlfriend were seen walking across a lovely garden, holding hands and acting affectionate while a bunch of circus performers jumped and dived and clowned around them. But in this new version the couple were walking in a graveyard and they were surrounded by an almost uncountable variety of ghosts, vampires, zombies, witches and werewolves. These ghoulish creatures all stared into the camera as it went by them and they all said something, but the music drowned out their words. Donald wasn't a good lip reader and he couldn't make out what they were saying, except he was pretty sure that the last word they all said was "Liar!" He decided, when the video ended, that he liked the original version a lot more.

He finished his dinner, turned off the TV and got up to go to his room so he could do some writing. He turned on his computer and waited for it to boot up as he tried to think of a new story to work on. He had just finished the last one he had started, and he didn't really have any ideas about what to do next. When a block like this happened to him he liked to try something he called Zen writing, which was to just write some sentences and see if they led him anywhere. Some of his best stories had been plucked right out of nowhere this way, so he saw no reason not to try it now.

When his computer was ready he clicked on his word processing program and closed his eyes for a minute to think of a first sentence. Since this was Zen writing, it could be almost anything, so—with his eyes still closed—he typed the first sentence that appeared in his head, which was "The sun rose high over the mountains."

He opened his eyes and looked at the screen and was shocked to see instead "We know what you are doing Donald and we want you to stop it!"

Confused, Donald deleted this sentence and tried to retype the one that was in his head. With his eyes open this time he was stunned to see himself type something just as disturbing:

"We will not be ignored! You have exploited us for too long and we will not let it continue any longer!"

Donald jumped up from his seat with a frightened shout. He looked down at his hands to see if something was wrong with them that would make them type these words out of some sort of random impulse. They looked fine. With a shudder he turned off his computer and started pacing in his room as he tried to figure out what was going on. Usually during stressful moments in his life, Donald liked to get in a bathtub and soak his worries away, so he stripped out of his clothes, grabbed a robe and went into his bathroom. He filled the tub up with hot water and then—as he always did—he turned off the lights, as he found the darkness peaceful and relaxing. He got in the tub and soaked for a good hour as he tried to comprehend what had just happened to him. The only explanation he could come up with was that a thought from deep in his unconscious was trying to come to the surface, but given what he had just written he had no clue what that thought could be.

The water started to grow cold, so he pulled the plug out with his big toe and stood up to get out of the tub. While he was up, he switched on the light and screamed. A cold dead hand grabbed him by the throat, lifted him out of the tub and slammed him hard against the back of his bathroom door. It cracked from the impact, and Donald flailed and kicked as the rotting figure that held him began to speak.

"Do you know who I am?" asked the dead man.

Donald was being choked too hard to answer vocally, so he shook his head instead.

"My name is Zephaniah Bogart!"

With that he dropped Donald, who fell to his feet, then turned and opened the bathroom door and ran out into his apartment's hallway, still naked and dripping wet. He didn't get far. Another ghoulish figure, this one a woman, blocked his path. Although obviously dead, she was still quite beautiful with pale skin, dark black hair and blood red lips. She wore a dark dress that looked almost like a monk's robe. Donald instinctively tried to cover himself up in front of her.

"Don't bother, *little* man," she mocked him, her voice sounding frosty and Southern.

Donald turned away from her and was confronted by another figure, a little girl whose clothes were shredded and cut as if she had been caught in some kind of machine. Her eyes were as black as ebony and she spoke matter-of-factly.

"We want to talk to you," she told him.

Donald dived to his right, out of the hallway and into his bedroom. He closed the door and pressed himself against it.

"That's not going to help," a sullen voice explained to him.

He turned around and saw a teenage girl who was dressed like a punk rocker.

"What do you want?" he pleaded with her.

The girl shrugged. "You heard the kid. We want to talk. And do you mind putting some clothes on? That's just gross."

This all proved too much for Donald to take. His eyes rolled to the back of his head, and his body fell forward in an unconscious heap.

When he woke up he was surrounded by close to a dozen different figures. All of them were obviously dead, and they were all in some way familiar. At some point they had picked him up and put his robe on him and placed him on his bed. Even though it was hot in his apartment, his whole body shivered. He looked up and saw that these more physical spirits were joined by less tangible ones who floated above them.

"You cannot get away from us, Donald," the beautiful Southern woman said to him, "so just sit there and listen. We all want to speak to you."

Donald just sat there on his bed and tried not to cry.

The little girl with the freaky black eyes stepped towards him. "You lied about me," she told him.

"I don't understand," Donald answered.

The old dead prospector spoke up. "You've lied about *all* of us. You wrote that I was married and that I dragged my wife with me into my grave." He pointed to the punk rock girl. "And you wrote that she slit her wrists rather than go to boarding school—"

"When I actually died of an asthma attack," the girl finished.

"You said I died hanging from a Yankee rope," said the Southern woman. She lifted up her head and ran her fingers down her long neck. "Do you *see* any rope burns here?"

One by one the figures around him told Donald all about the lies he had written.

"How would you feel," asked Zephaniah when everyone had spoken, "if someone wrote a story that said you were a no-account scoundrel who didn't know an honest thought from a hole in the ground?"

"He'd feel fine," the Southern woman answered, "because that would be the *truth*."

"I'm sorry," Donald apologized to them all.

"We don't want your *sorry!*" Zephaniah shouted at him.

"Then what do you want?" asked Donald as his heart raced.

"We want the truth!" they all shouted at him.

"I don't know what that means," answered Donald.

"It means," the punk girl told him, "that you are going to rewrite all our stories."

"But properly this time!" barked Zephaniah.

Donald felt almost relieved. "Is that all? I can do that. I can rewrite a dozen or so stories, no problem."

This made them laugh.

"What's so funny?" he asked them.

"You don't think we're the only ones angry with you, do you?" laughed Zephaniah. "Hell, every ghost you've written about is ready to string you up for what you said about them."

"This is a small apartment," the Southern woman explained. "There is no way all of us could have fit in here."

"But I've written hundreds of stories," Donald protested.

"That's right," answered the little girl, "you've written hundreds of lies."

Donald's mind boggled at the idea of rewriting every ghost story he had written, but it still did not feel like an impossible task.

"Fine," he said to them. "I can do it, no problem."

"Sure you can," Zephaniah sneered at him, "and we're going to stay here and make sure you do it right!"

"What do you mean?"

"He means," the Southern woman told him, "that we are going to stay with you until you finish all the stories."

"And," the punk girl continued, "we're going to decide if what you write is good enough to do us justice. If it isn't, you're going to have to do it again."

Donald grew very pale. "You guys are going to be my editors?"

"That's right!" they answered.

Donald didn't come into the office the next day. No one said anything, assuming that he must be doing research somewhere or working at home, but when no one heard from him for two weeks, it became clear that something was wrong. He didn't answer his calls or emails, and it seemed as if he had just vanished.

Another week passed before Donald's neighbors complained about the strong smell that was coming out of his apartment. The landlord used his key to get in and was almost overpowered by the stench that hit him. To his horror he found Donald hanging from a rope in his room. Pinned to him was a note that simply read "Too many critics."

To fill his absence the company hired a new writer named Howard, and he took over Donald's cubicle. By a strange coincidence a young woman named Darcy, who was a casual acquaintance of Howard's, moved into his predecessor's apartment, despite its morbid history. She had lived there for two years when she saw Howard at a party and told him about how her apartment seemed to be haunted. She told him how late at night she could hear the sound of typing coming from her computer, along with a murmur of disapproving whispers. Howard liked her story, so he wrote it and put it into one of his books, but instead of having Donald commit suicide he changed it so the young writer died of a brain embolism while finishing up the last chapter of his first novel. He thought this made the story less depressing and served as a good explanation for Donald's ghostly writing from beyond.

And even though Donald didn't approve of Howard's taking liberties with the story of his death, he was far too busy to do anything about it.

A Voice in the Dark

It was the pain in her right leg that brought Melissa back to the waking world. Slowly her eyes opened, and she found that she could see just as much with them closed. The darkness was heavy and absolute, and it took her some time to figure out what had happened.

She remembered sitting in the doctor's office at eight that morning. She had been so excited—all the signs pointed to a complete remission, and she had looked forward to what she was sure was going to be good news. She had also been anxious, afraid that her optimism was misguided and that the leukemia she had spent so much time fighting had somehow managed to remain inside her. She couldn't concentrate and wasn't able to read any of the old magazines that sat on the table in front of her. Out of nervous habit her right leg shook up and down and caused her chair and the others around it to gently vibrate. It was then, as if her anxiety could be felt by the earth below, that the vibration grew, and soon the whole building began to shake.

Melissa had spent her entire life in California and was used to the earthquakes that famously plagued the state, so when it became clear that another one was happening, her first reaction wasn't fear but annoyance that her appointment would probably be delayed. She wasn't alone. Everybody in the waiting room raised their eyebrows and smiled conspiratorially in a way that expressed their solidarity as Los Angelenos.

But as the building rattled and bumped, it soon became clear that this wasn't any normal afternoon seismic yawn, but instead an angry and destructive roar. The calm demeanor of Melissa and those around her quickly faded when they realized that this one was serious. The furniture jumped and light fixtures fell from the ceiling. Everyone ran for cover as the floor began to twist and buckle. Melissa found herself alone in the doorway to her doctor's private office. As she crouched down, she wondered where Dr. Yakamoto was. He was the man who had treated her illness, and she so respected his skills as a lifesaver that a part of her genuinely believed that if anyone could stop the earthquake, he could. As the building's metal frame screamed and twisted, she put her hands to her ears and closed her eyes.

She had felt herself fall and that was the last thing she remembered before the sharp, throbbing, constant pain in her right leg jolted her back into reality, surrounded by the remains of the building and the terrifying darkness.

She was on her back and had very little room to maneuver. She tried her best to use her hands to explore her surroundings, but all they did was warn her to stay away from the sharp, jagged edges that were all around her. There wasn't enough room for her to sit up, so she couldn't get her hands to where her leg hurt. It felt as though something heavy was on it, but she didn't know what. She tried to move it, but the pain that rocketed through her body made it clear that her best option was to stay as still as possible. As she lay there, she did her best to listen to what was happening around her, but all she heard were the same sounds of silence that were familiar to her from lying in bed at night when she was unable to sleep. She remembered all the other people who had been in the waiting room with her, and she wondered if any of them were in the same situation. She kept quiet for as long as she could, afraid that if she spoke she might cause the small pocket around her to collapse, but finally she couldn't take it anymore and she began to shout.

"Hello! Is anyone there? Can anyone hear me?"

Her voice echoed in her small space, and she waited for a response, but none came. She tried again.

"Is anyone out there? Please! I'm scared and I don't want to be alone." Melissa began to cry. "If you can hear me, please say something. It's so dark and I can't move and my leg hurts. I need to hear someone's voice. I need to know that I'm going to be okay."

Melissa couldn't move her arms enough to wipe away her tears, so she felt them as they stung her cheeks and fell down the side of her face and into her hair.

"Melissa?"

She heard a voice, buried in the distance, but still clear enough that she could make it out. It was a voice she knew. It was the voice she respected above any other.

"Dr. Yakamoto?" she cried with relief. "Is that you? Are you okay?"

"I've been better, but I can't complain," the voice responded. Even in this dire situation, Dr. Yakamoto was still capable of making Melissa laugh, which she did gratefully as her tears of fear and pain turned into tears of joy. "How about you?"

"I'm a bit scared right now." Melissa's voice shook with emotion.

"Really? How come?" He spoke conversationally, feigning innocence to help keep her calm.

"Because we're trapped in the rubble of a collapsed building." She did her best to sound as nonchalant as he did.

"Oh, right. Not the best way to spend a day, huh?"

"No."

"You said something about your leg?"

"It hurts. I think something may be on top of it, but I can't tell."

"What's the pain like? Is it worse than chemo?"

"Nothing's worse than chemo."

"That's right. Remember that. As bad as this may be, just think about how much better it is than going through chemo again."

Melissa took her doctor's advice and imagined going through chemotherapy for a third time. The thought of it made her present situation seem like a holiday in comparison. One of the things she loved about Dr. Yakamoto was that no matter how dark things seemed to be, he always managed to remain optimistic and find the positive light. Over the past few years Melissa had come to rely on this trait. A year before her diagnosis, her parents had been killed in a car accident, leaving her without anybody to provide emotional support. Dr. Yakamoto had filled that void. Not only did he spend time talking with her, but he also made her a part of his family, inviting her over for the holidays and his children's birthdays. In the beginning Melissa had felt guilty, afraid that she was inconveniencing him, but he quickly dismissed this idea the one time she brought it up.

"I'm a doctor," he had told her. "It is my job to make my patients well again. To do that I must be certain that they feel loved, because if they don't then there is little for them to live for. Most of my patients have families who take care of this for me, but in your case I have to do it myself. I consider that an honor, not a burden, so don't you worry about it a second longer. Worrying causes anxiety and anxious people are barely able to survive hiccups, much less leukemia. Now get out of here before I get all weepy."

"Melissa?" The doctor's voice interrupted her memories.

"Yes, doctor?"

"I've got some good news and some bad news. What do you want to hear first?"

Whenever he gave her this option, she always chose to start with the bad. This time wasn't any different.

"The bad news always makes the good that much sweeter," she answered, parroting a phrase she had heard him say many times before.

"Well, the bad news is that you could be stuck here for quite some time."

Melissa took a deep breath and prayed that somehow the good news could triumph over the bad.

She spoke hesitantly. "And the good news?"

"When they do find you they'll find someone who is in complete remission."

Hearing this and what it meant overpowered Melissa and rendered her speechless, as her eyes once again grew heavy with tears.

"Hello? Are you still there?" Dr. Yakamoto called out, sounding worried by her silence.

"Yes," she managed. "Yes, I am."

"In hindsight it would have been a lot better if I'd just told you over the phone, but I wanted to see your face when you found out. Kind of selfish, really. I'm sorry."

"That's okay."

"You did it!" he told her, pride evident in his voice. "You beat it!"

"We beat it," she corrected him.

"No. It was all you. I was just the coach who made sure you ran all your laps. You're the one who won the race."

"That's not true."

"Yes it is, Melissa. Do you know how strong that makes you? You beat cancer! You kicked its butt and threw it out your door. Are you listening to me?"

"Uh-huh."

"Good, because it's important that you hear this. You're in a very scary situation right now. Most people wouldn't be able to handle it, but that's because they're not strong, like you. You're a fighter and compared to cancer this is just a head cold, so I want you to stay calm and remember that. You are going to be okay. It may take awhile and it may seem hopeless at times, but I assure you that it will end and you will have a whole lifetime to live after it's done. Okay?"

There was something about the certainty with which he spoke that convinced her that he was telling the truth and not just something he thought she needed to hear.

"Okay," she answered.

"All right then. Now, since we have some time to kill, I'm thinking of a famous historical personality. I'll give you 20 questions to guess who it is."

Together the two of them did their best to pass the time by playing games and telling jokes. Dr. Yakamoto told Melissa all about his life, starting with his early childhood in Japan, before going on to the difficult adjustment that was America. She in turn told him all about her parents and how much she missed them. He told her that they were proud of her, and he said it with such conviction that it sounded as if they had told him so personally.

As they spoke Melissa lost all sense of time. She had no idea how long they had been trapped underneath the rubble. It could just as easily have been hours as days. At several points she had fallen asleep, but the only other signs she had to go by were the hunger and thirst that had overtaken her body and mind. Her stomach growled, while her mouth and throat turned to cotton. Her voice grew raspy, but Dr. Yakamoto's remained unaffected. Eventually she could barely speak above a whisper, but he still somehow managed to hear her and did his best to keep her talking.

But soon she found it difficult to keep track of what he was saying. She faded in and out of consciousness and found it almost impossible to concentrate. She no longer felt any pain.

"Fight, Melissa! You're stronger than this! All you have to do is stay alive a little longer! They're coming! You just have to wait for them! You just have to wait!" They were the last words she heard him speak.

Surrounded by the darkness, Melissa dreamed of her parents. They smiled at her and opened their arms. She ran to them, but before she could join them in the warm embrace she had missed so much since they died, she felt a hand grab her by the waist of her pants. Despite her protests it began to drag her away. She turned her head and saw the familiar sight of her favorite doctor.

"Not now" was all he had to say.

He dragged her back to the edge of her mind and pushed her back into the waking world. Her eyes opened and she saw a tiny pinprick of light. Overhead she heard the sounds of men working. The pinprick grew bigger and bigger. She heard a voice.

"I think I see someone!"

She tried to say something, to let them know that she was there, but her voice was so quiet she herself couldn't hear it.

The pinprick grew to be the size of a small plate and through it she saw a head poke through.

"There's definitely someone down there!"

Slowly the light around her began to grow. She saw the bodies of men in heavy raincoats and yellow helmets standing above her. The light hurt her eyes, so she kept them closed. She felt the weight that had been pressing down on her right leg lift away, and then she felt the touch of gloved hands grab her. As the men lifted her out, she tried to speak once again, but her words were drowned out by the shock expressed by her rescuers.

"She's alive! Oh my God, she's alive!" one of them shouted, as if it was a miracle.

She tried to speak and tell them about the man buried somewhere below her, but they couldn't understand her and they were too busy working to keep her alive to pay attention. Finally her strength gave out. She grew silent and fell into a very deep sleep.

She did not dream as she slept, so her mind was as dark and black as the hell from which she had just been rescued, but this time the darkness was warm and comforting and she felt safe. She stayed there for a while, until finally she decided she had had enough and illuminated the darkness by opening her eyes. She felt weak and found it difficult to make out what was happening around her, but she couldn't help noticing that a lot of excited-looking people kept coming up to her. She observed them quietly for a while before she found the strength to ask what was going on. This caused even more excitement and eventually Melissa found herself face to face with a smallish woman in her 30s who talked with a calm and steady voice.

"Melissa," the woman said, "my name is Dr. Lori Davies. Do you know where you are?"

"A hospital?" Melissa answered quietly, having worked out the clues.

"That's right," Dr. Davies nodded. "Do you know why?"

"Trapped," Melissa said recalling her nightmare. "The earthquake."

"Right again, Melissa," the doctor smiled. "You're a very lucky woman. Do you know that?"

"Lucky?" Melissa's voice was dry and brittle, and it bore the inflection of someone who almost didn't understand the word.

"Very lucky. Do you know how long you were down there?"

Melissa shook her head.

"Two days?" she guessed.

Dr. Davies shook her head.

"You were down there for a week, Melissa. Without food or water. You should be dead. The newspapers are calling you a miracle, and I can't disagree."

"A week?" Melissa could not believe it.

"By the time you were found, it was no longer considered a rescue operation because it was assumed that everyone still inside the rubble would have died by then. No one knows how you did it, but you proved them wrong."

"*We* proved them wrong," Melissa said.

"Excuse me?"

"We did," Melissa insisted. "Dr. Yakamoto was just below me. He kept talking to me. That's how I know he's alive."

Dr. Davies looked down for a moment before she spoke again.

"Melissa," she said, her voice still calm but not as steady. "I cannot comprehend what happened to you, and it would be wrong for me to tell you what you did or did not hear when you were down there, but I can tell you that Dr. Yakamoto did not survive the earthquake."

"But he was right below me," Melissa argued. "I could hear him and he sounded much stronger than I did."

"Melissa, I know the Yakamotos. Akira's wife, Janice, is a good friend of mine, and that's why I know that he was late to work on the day of the earthquake. When it hit he was still in his car. A streetlight fell over and crashed onto his roof. He died instantly. He wasn't in the building when it collapsed."

Melissa didn't say a word. Dr. Davies went on to explain how they had managed to save her leg, which in itself constituted another miracle, but Melissa didn't hear her. Instead she closed her eyes and thought of the voice that had kept her sane throughout her ordeal and that had insisted she had the strength to endure it. She heard it again and she had no doubt. She had not imagined it. Dr. Yakamoto had once again gone beyond the call of duty to help save her life.

Now, it occurred to her, she owed it to him to live it.

GHOST
HOUSE